Tilabrook Tales

by
Jack Ruth
Dobie Hill
Ted Houlahan Comerford

Level HeΛding

To the memory of Doctor Bomford,
the nurses and people of the
Bendigo Psychiatric Centre:
friends and benefactors.

Acknowledgements

To my sister Beverley for financing this project and
my brother Sim for his illustrations.

Tilabrook Tales was first written
between 1974 and 1978. The front cover
illustration was drawn in 1976 and the
back cover was done about 1974.

Pioneering tales of Aboriginal Yurgama Jacobs
and his dingo pet Marakorpa.

Yurgama was the resident Trooper in the
Victorian town of Tilabrook, where he kept
law and order with the aid of his steel-rimmed
boomerang.

The black Trooper of Tilabrook
was the enemy of every bushranger and crook.
Yurgama Jacobs was his name
And peace and justice were his aim.
Good people were protected by Yurgama,
While the bad were captured with the aid of his arkana.
And as well as battling with people who were shady,
Yurgama loved a pretty lady.

Contents

Introduction

An exploration party of whites came upon a small tribe of Aborigines in Victoria. The whites offered gifts to the natives, but they misunderstood the foreigners' desire to be friendly.

Hence, a tragic skirmish ensued. The natives fighting with spears and the whites defending with guns caused the fall of the blacks.

When they saw their menfolk go down, the women of the tribe took up the fight. The result was that the white party had a few members with minor wounds, while the blacks were virtually wiped out.

Henry Jacobs, one of the white party, went about the fallen blacks in a last compassionate gesture. He offered a water bottle to a dying native woman. She pushed the bottle away, pointed and gasped, "Yurgama! Yurgama!".

Her signal was directed towards her small infant boy, who was crawling towards a smouldering fire. Henry Jacobs saved the child and took him home to his wife. They called the baby Yurgama and raised him.

When he left school, Yurgama did missionary work among tribal Aborigines. From a native, he learnt how to make and throw a boomerang.

Later, he worked in a metal foundry where he got the idea

to make an arkana or boomerang with a sharp steel rim on its inside. At first, he had difficulty controlling the use of his implement, which he found could be dangerous. But eventually he mastered throwing it and found he could do tricks with it.

At this time, Henry Jacob's health was failing. In order to pay for better medical treatment for his ailing foster father, Yurgama joined a circus and did stunts with his boomerang. However, Henry Jacobs died and the Aborigine's foster mother, Mrs Eunice Jacobs, passed on soon afterwards.

Yurgama felt the loss of his foster parents, but he continued with the circus.

When a German trapeze artist, Hans Erhard, had a disagreement with the circus manager, the artist tried to kill the manager's daughter. He coaxed her to go up to the tent top with him and have a try at swinging on the bar. The girl realised there was no net below and wanted to climb down. Immediately, Erhard began swinging on the trapeze, attempting to knock her off the platform.

Other members of the circus came from everywhere when they heard her screams. Yurgama began throwing the steel-rimmed boomerang at the ropes on which the German swung.

Some throws missed, but other throws cut into the ropes, and eventually Erhard fell to the ground to his death.

As a result of this incident, Yurgama was persuaded to join the Colonial Police Force. At first he acted as a plain-clothes upholder of the law. For a time, he was stationed as assistant Trooper at the town of Bolangatta in South Australia. Then he became resident Trooper of the Tilabrook district in northern Victoria.

In the country area of Tilabrook, a shepherd came across a young dingo pup below a fairly steep ridge. The pup's front left leg was broken and it was in pain.

The shepherd surmised that the young animal must have fallen from the ridge. He took it to the Tilabrook medical practitioner, Doctor Eric Wudder. Doctor Wudder decided that the dingo's leg would have to be amputated. With skill which a veterinary surgeon would have complimented him, he carried out the operation and the animal recovered.

The shepherd gave the pup to Yurgama to have as a pet and he called the now three-legged dingo, Marakorpa.

The word *yurgama* is Aboriginal for quick or quickly. *Marakorpa* is a Tasmanian Aboriginal word meaning handsome.

The black trooper was six feet tall and weighed fourteen stone. His chestnut stallion was seventeen hands.

When he threw the arkana, and wanted it to cut through an intended target, the Aborigine would have the thumb of his throwing hand on the steel rim of the boomerang. When he wanted the back of the implement to hit a target, he put his thumb on the wood of the weapon. Then a different spin would be generated on the arkana in its flight, ensuring that the back of it truck the intended object or target.

My Heart Lies in New Zealand

Aboriginal Trooper Yurgama Jacobs, strolled casually into the Magpie Hotel in Tilabrook, northern Victoria, leaving his three-legged dingo pet, Marakorpa, who obediently waited outside for his Master's return.

The bearded black Trooper's attention was drawn to a young lady who was the only person present in the Hotel's Public Bar in this early hour of the morning. Seeing the pretty girl caused the Aborigine to step towards her, not because she was pretty, but because of her Polynesian appearance. She was dressed in European clothes, but she had long black, plaited hair, brown skin and a colourful band around her forehead.

In a dingy, irregularly cleaned corner that wasn't as frequently used by the public as other parts of the bar, the girl sat burrowing into a handbag.

Looking closer, Yurgama noticed a large spider that was weaving a web and was only inches above the young lady's head. He took his steel-rimmed boomerang from his belt and threw it. The sharp steel on the inside of the curved flat piece of wood, in its transit, struck the spider, which fell to the floor dead.

The lass looked up with shock as the boomerang returned to land at the Aborigine's feet in its flight.

"What's happened?" she cried as he picked up his implement.

The Trooper gave his explanation and the young lady was pleased to answer his inquisitive questions about her which followed.

Her name was Maru, she was a Maori from Whakarewarewa village, Rotorua, in the North Island of New Zealand. She had come to Australia to see her missing fiancé, Paul Wines, the son of the Anglican Missionary of Whakarewarewa. Wines had left New Zealand without anyone's knowledge. A mutual friend of the couple, Simon Bechmore, who had made a lot of money from kauri gum digging, accompanied Maru to Australia and financed her voyage.

Maru asked Yurgama about himself and when the Aborigine mentioned Marakorpa, the girl wanted to see his pet. The reddish yellow dingo with its front left leg missing, enjoyed the young lady's patting. She learnt from the Aborigine that his pet's leg had to be amputated because of an accident it had when it was a pup. The only complaint he had about the animal was that it had gotten into the recent bad habit of wandering.

When Yurgama left Maru, he was puzzled. The Maori girl told him that her friend Bechmore had found out that Paul Wines was living on a small sheep grazing property three miles west of Tilabrook. Bechmore was taking her there, but as far as the black Trooper knew, an old shepherd lived on the particular property. Apparently, the shepherd must have sold out to Maru's fiancé.

Simon Bechmore, a bald-headed, bushy-bearded, gruff looking man, drove the expectant, excited young lady out to the place in a wagon. But upon arrival at the humble homestead of the property, a broken down mud house, there was no-one about.

Maru became more and more suspicious as Bechmore evaded her questions and only spoke of how they could improve the appearance of the house together. At last it occurred to the girl that she had been tricked; that Bechmore had designs on her. She accused him and he reacted with pleasant deceit, till she spat in his face after he went to take her in his arms.

The angry man grabbed her hair and jerked her head back, causing Maru's brown eyes to well with tears from the pain.

When she warned: "if Paul ever finds out what you've done to me, Simon". Bechmore scornfully announced that her fiancé had married a wealthy Queensland squatter's daughter.

Maru did not want to believe his claim, and her predicament with him did not make her feel any better. He reminded her that she had no friends and no money in this foreign country. He said that he would keep her prisoner till she submitted to him.

But hope dismissed despair. The Maori girl discovered Marakorpa sniffing around the front of the mud house later, when Bechmore was fortunately unharnessing the horse from the wagon out the back. The dingo must have followed the wagon. Hurriedly, Maru wrote a note asking Yurgama to come to her rescue and she slipped it inside his pet's collar.

By the end of the day, after he had chopped a lot of wood, Bechmore sat down, rolled a cigarette and called out to the forlorn Maori girl to come outside and talk to him.

When Maru came out, he dismayed her by remarking that a three-legged dog had been around the place earlier in the day. But the girl's spirits lifted slightly when her abductor continued to say he had to throw a couple of stones at the dog to chase it away.

"You be a good girl, Maru. We can make a home here and I

will take care of you," he said, lighting his cigarette.

"Give me a smile!" he suggested. "Come and sit beside me!"

"No!" refused the lass loudly.

Bechmore got up and went to her tauntingly.

"Nobody knows you're here, my dear, and they won't find out."

"I despise you," declared Maru defiantly. Bechmore grabbed her arm, twisted it and raised his cigarette in the air saying he was going to burn her with it.

The Maori girl incited him to carry out his threat when she attempted to kick him.

But before Bechmore could cause the young lady any further pain, the raised cigarette was cut in half by Yurgama's steel-rimmed boomerang. He had arrived on the scene and thrown his steel-rimmed implement which he put back inside his belt after it returned to land at his feet.

"I found your note on Korpa when he came back, Maru. I rode as fast as I could," indicated the black Trooper.

"Who are you starless night?" asked Bechmore disdainfully of the Aborigine.

"Yurgama ordered him to let Maru go. The bald-headed man obliged, but he immediately picked up the axe he had used to chop the wood.

"I'm afraid your presence has presented a problem to me, Trooper, and I'll have to put you out of the way. So I'm going to kill you. I'm going to have to chop you up," declared Bechmore.

A horrified Maru stood helpless as her abductor took swing after swing with the axe at the dodging, retreating Trooper.

Soon Yurgama literally had his back against the wall of the mud house. His position was dangerous. He had to defend himself.

Bechmore thought he had the Trooper at his mercy. Desperately, Yurgama whipped his boomerang from his belt and belted it into the side of his assailant's neck. The sharp steel cut deeply. Bechmore let out a piercing yell and collapsed.

Before the Aborigine could think of helping him, the Maori girl ran straight to his arms. Yurgama needed her close to him, just as much as she needed him, after the traumatic experience.

They were unable to save Bechmore's life.

After much effort and many inquiries, the black Trooper was able to find the changed whereabouts of the old shepherd, who lived at the mud house. He had sold his wagon, horse and property to Bechmore for a price which he declared, "was too good to turn down".

To Maru's disappointment, the Shepherd confirmed her abductor's claim that Paul Wines had married. He met Wines when he first came to Australia and the Maori girl's fiancé boasted he had won a large amount of money from Bechmore to jilt her. Wines intention after that was to wed a Queensland lass.

The shepherd was emphatic that he did not know Bechmore had come to Australia with Maru, however.

The Aborigine gently spoke to the Maori girl. "Maru, you've been hurt. If it's possible, I'd like to heal that hurt. I'd like to be your friend. Dr Eric Wudder, our Medical Practitioner has a need of an assistant. The mere sight of you would cheer up his patients. Why don't you stay in Tilabrook?"

"No, Yurgama. It's very kind of you. But my heart lies in New Zealand. If Doctor Wudder will have me, I will accept his position until I can save enough money to return home," replied the lass.

"Well, Korpa will miss you," remarked the Trooper as the tail-wagging dingo nuzzled up to her.

"Thank goodness he has gotten into the recent bad habit of wandering," added the relieved young lady.

"I'd certainly have to admit that," agreed the Aborigine.

Home for the Koalas

The drawing room of the Dibson's bluestone homestead at Mount Alexander was alive with much talking among the family. Murray Dibson had settled with his wife and daughter Kathleen at Mount Alexander, which was about seventy-five miles north of Melbourne. He provided for his family by grazing Hereford cattle and Corriedale sheep on a five hundred acre property.

Freckle-faced eleven-year-old Kathleen was contributing the most conversation to the family conference. She informed her parents that a former Castlemaine gold seeker had bought bushland at Mount Alexander from the Victorian Government; that he intended to clear the bush to sow grass and graze stock. She complained because the particular land was part of an area which was full of koalas and they could be endangered. Kathleen told her parents she approached the Castlemaine man, a Mr Ian Coakley, and tried to persuade him to transfer the koalas out of the land he had bought to surrounding parts of Mount Alexander, before he instructed his hired timbermen to clear his land. Coakley refused, saying he needed all the money he could get and that the furs of any koalas killed on his property would mean more money. The freckle-faced girl wanted her father to approach the Castlemaine man, but

Murray Dibson felt his persuasive powers would fail to make an impression too.

It was a warm summery night and the Dibson's had Yurgama and Marakorpa staying with them. Yurgama had insisted on washing the dishes from the evening meal and in the bluestone kitchen, he could clearly hear the loud talk from the drawing room. A hungry Marakorpa managed to press his nose between the handle of the backdoor to the kitchen, open it and make his way in. Immediately, his Aboriginal master showed him the way out, but he put down before the appreciative dingo a hearty bowl of Irish stew scraps that had been left over from the evening meal.

By this time, Kathleen Dibson was almost demanding her father to buy Coakley's land from him to save the koalas.

In an attempt to be of assistance, Yurgama later told the lass he would approach the Castlemaine man in the morning, but he was not confident he could do any good either.

During a beautiful sunrise, the Tilabrook Trooper walked two miles from the Dibson homestead before he reached Coakley's camp. Marakorpa romped along as well—stopping periodically to investigate anything he considered interesting.

At the camp, where tents were erected, a few genial fellows greeted the Aborigine. They were the Castlemaine man's employees. They said their boss was away, but that he shouldn't be too long and would Yurgama like to wait for his return. The Aborigine accepted the friendly suggestion.

The men offered him tea. But when the black Trooper received a tin mug of the beverage and went to take a sip, he noticed one ginger-haired fellow trying to poke a stick at a nest suspended from the branch of a manna gum. The nest was made of wood fibres mixed with saliva and it must have aroused the man's curiosity. But the Aborigine saw that the fellow could be in danger. The Trooper dropped his tea mug, whipped his boomerang from his belt and threw it. In its flight the sharp steel in the implement cut the stick in half. Before anyone present could express their surprise at the unannounced action, Yurgama picked up his boomerang when it returned to land at his feet and threw it again.

On the second throw, the weapon struck an insect that appeared hovering above the puzzled ginger-haired fellow's head. When his implement returned to his feet again, Yurgama, with everyone else, examined the insect he had killed. It was a red paper nest wasp. Three pairs of eyes of those present riveted onto the Aborigine as if they wanted an explanation for his actions. He explained that the paper nest wasp is extremely aggressive and stings without provocation. He felt that the ginger-haired fellow would certainly have been bitten.

The men marvelled because Yurgama was at least twenty yards away when he threw his boomerang. However, he was quick to say he did not expect to strike the wasp with his weapon. It was complete good fortune.

The Trooper waited two hours for Coakley, but he never returned. So the Aborigine decided to go back to the Dibsons.

Then, when he was strolling through some open bushland a while later, he came across a precise looking little man, who was going to shoot at something with a rifle. To Yurgama's shock, the man seemed to be aiming at Marakorpa. Immediately, the Aborigine threw his boomerang and part of its steel rim wedged into the man's firearm. The little fellow dropped the gun aghast and angry.

"That contraption landed near my wrist, Mister. You could maim or kill someone with it," he declared.

Apologising, the Aborigine told the fellow he thought he was shooting at his pet. The little fellow made his own apology saying he recognised that Marakorpa was a dingo and he heard they were a menace to sheep squatters.

But the stranger's friendliness soon reverted back to his original anger, when he introduced himself as being Ian Coakley and learnt why Yurgama wanted to see him. He departed abruptly from the Aborigine after returning his boomerang to him.

However, as he went on his incensed way, Coakley was halted in his stride by a whimpering sound. He discovered it belonged to a little greyish-brown animal with a yellowish bottom, rounded fury ears and a leathery expanded almost trunk-like nose. It was a baby koala and the Castlemaine man surmised that it must have fallen from a nearby tree, because the animal was nearly dead.

He carried it to his camp and tried to give it food and much gentle attention. But the little koala died.

However, the experience caused Ian Coakley to go to the Dibsons later. At the bluestone homestead, he informed Kathleen that he was going to give his timbermen employees the task of transferring all the koalas from his land, before he had them clear it.

"Oh, Mr Coakley, I could kiss you! In fact I will," was the reaction of the freckle-faced young lass and she gave him a hug as well as a peck on the cheek.

"Now, none of that, girlie. You embarrass me," commented the uncomfortable little Castlemaine man.

"I'd given up hope for the koalas when Yurgama came back and said he failed to persuade you to save them," remarked Kathleen.

"Do you know what changed my mind?" said Coakley.

"I think so. Seeing that little one in distress you told me about, touched your heart," suggested the girl.

"Yes," stated the former gold seeker. And someday there may be a law that will protect all koalas throughout the country, Kathleen."

"Do you really think so?" asked the lass with gladness.

"Yes, I'm confidently sure of it," emphasised the Castlemaine man.

Hold Me Forever

Nigel Exert was a farmer in the complete sense of the word. On his rich land in the Tilabrook district, he ran sheep, cattle, pigs, turkeys and fowls. After his first wife died, he was left on his own to rear their only child, Michael. The farmer was lonely, but this sadness ended after he remarried.

When he left school, Michael left his father and step-mother Zelda and the bush, to find his niche in the city life in Melbourne.

It was a late Sunday morning in mid winter.

Even though the weather was overcast and cold, the solidly built, fair-haired, middle-aged Nigel Exert whistled gaily as he walked to his red brick house after feeding his poultry. Over the back porch of the home he passed his old faithful black kelpie, "Ferocious", who looked up at him with sad eyes. "Ferocious" was a moody canine and the fair-haired farmer was the only person who could touch him without the dog growling.

Inside his house, in the kitchen, Nigel, with a warm kiss, greeted his big blue-eyed, brown-haired, tall, beautiful looking wife Zelda. She had just baked a fruit cake and was putting it out to cool on a bench.

Her happy husband declared, "I feel on top of the world this morning, Darling. This day, seven years ago, we were married."

The man's wife looked uneasy. "Oh, I'd forgotten," she said unenthusiastically.

"They have been wonderful years for me, Zelda. And it's all because of you," continued the farmer.

"Nigel, it's horrible of me to say what I'm going to say—especially today of all days."

"What's the matter, dear?"

"I'm glad I've made you happy," started the attractive woman.

"But you're not happy?" asked her shocked husband. He put his hands on her shoulders. "Have I failed you?"

"No, not at all. You're a good man. But I don't know whether I love you. I don't know whether I ever loved you, or just felt sorry for you after you lost your first wife."

"But you've been married to me for so long. I never knew you had such bottled-up feelings. Have you felt like this very long?"

"On and off—almost from the moment I agreed to your proposal. Repeatedly through the years, I've wanted to tell you what I've just told you. But you have been so devoted to me. You have done your best for me and I never had the heart to want to hurt you. But recently, I've felt I couldn't go on any longer."

The farmer let his hands drop from his wife's shoulders to his sides. "What do you want to do?" he asked quietly.

"Go and live with Mum and Dad."

"All right, I'll take you to the Cobb & Co depot in the morning. You can take the coach to Melbourne if you like?"

"Thanks for being so placid about it, Nigel. Once again, like always, you have done your best to make me happy."

"Is there another man, Zelda?"

"No."

An unpleasant silence pervaded for a few moments. With

some bitterness in his voice, Nigel Exert remarked: "it's funny, but I invited Yurgama Jacobs to have dinner with us today. You may remember, it was Yurgama who helped me to win you. He could be here any time now. I forgot to mention that I'd asked him out."

"Don't worry—I'll have enough food prepared," assured the man's wife with a smile.

He went into the living room of the home and slumped into an armchair close to a fire. He tried to read a newspaper so that he would not have to think about the shattering blow that had just befallen him. But he fell into an uneasy sleep.

Soon the noise of a horse's hooves trotting up the driveway could be heard. Zelda rushed out to greet the visitor as he dismounted from his chestnut stallion. It was Yurgama with Marakorpa who had his tongue out panting from keeping up with the horse on the journey.

"Hello Yurgama!" welcomed Zelda.

"Grateful to be able to come, Zelda," replied the Aborigine with a grin.

"I'm glad to see you have brought Korpa. He's such a lovely dog, isn't he," she continued. Then turning to Yurgama's pet, she slapped her thigh and beckoned it with a "come on, boy!"

Before the placid natured dingo could respond, "Ferocious" appeared and barked boisterously.

At first Marakorpa wanted to be friendly to the Exert's dog, But as soon as the reddish-yellow dingo sniffed "Ferocious" tail, the black kelpie reacted savagely. Fortunately, the fight that resulted was only temporary and neither dog got injured.

As Zelda showed the Aborigine into the living room to see Nigel, she expected to find a peaceful scene with her husband still sleeping.

He was still sleeping, but a log had rolled out of the fire. The farmer had a limp hold on his newspaper, over the side of the chair. But a corner of the paper was touching a part of the log that was alive with red ashes.

Before the paper could burst into flames, the black trooper whipped his boomerang from his belt and threw it. In its transit the steel cut the paper in half.

As the Aborigine's implement returned to his feet, Nigel Exert woke up and nonchalantly commented: "Yurgama, you've arrived! What are you throwing your stick around in here for?"

The two hosts did not expose the fact that they were going to separate. And their guest did not suspect the strain that pervaded between them.

During dinner in the Exert dining room, Yurgama from his position at the table, thought he saw something moving toward the fruit cake on the kitchen bench. He quietly excused himself to investigate and discovered a big grey rat. It was making its way along the edge of the bench towards the cake and was only a foot away from it. The Aborigine threw his boomerang, and in its flight, the steel cut deeply into the rodent which fell to the floor and died.

As the Trooper's boomerang returned to his feet, his hosts hurried out just in time to surmise what happened.

"You're really coming to the rescue today, Yurgama," declared an amused Zelda. "First you saved Nigel and now the fruit cake. You had better have a piece as a reward."

The next morning, as he had offered, the farmer took his wife in his gig, into the coach depot at Tilabrook.

The man concealed his melancholy by being determined to be cheerful to his wife. Instinctively, he felt she would prefer he did not wait to farewell her when the coach commenced the journey. Thus, with warm wishes of good luck to Zelda, he left her to wait for the stage to depart.

But about an hour later, while the farmer was getting some lunch in the kitchen of his home, he heard a commotion which sounded like the arrival of visitors. Before he could go out to investigate, someone rushed in.

"Zelda!" said the man aloud with shock. His wife went straight to him.

"Nigel, I was on the coach when it was about to leave. Then I saw our next door neighbour's wagon in the town. I frantically delayed the coach driver, to say I wasn't going on the trip. Our neighbours gave me a ride back here. I couldn't leave you. I'll never leave you. You're too nice. Hold me Darling! Hold me forever!"

Unforgettable Picnic

By a billabong near the Tarrola river in northern Victoria, Fedor and Oenone Cushing were having a picnic with Yurgama.

While Oenone boiled a billy for tea over a small fire, her husband and the black Trooper stood some distance away looking at two kookaburras laughing in a red gum. The men were discussing the characteristics of this type of bird. This led to Fedor suggesting to his friend, that they go for a short stroll while his wife prepared the food they had brought.

They turned around to ask Oenone if she would mind them leaving her, when the woman was about to take a sip of tea from a mug. Unexpectedly, Yurgama whipped his boomerang from his belt and threw it. Before returning to land at his feet, the curved implement knocked Oenone's mug out of her hand, splashing to the ground.

"What did you do that for Yurgama?" asked the shocked lady.

"This funnel web spider was on your mug, Love," showed her husband, stepping forward to put his foot on the eight-legged spider.

The two men took their walk, and during it, Fedor stopped the Trooper to point out something he saw. It was a rabbit sitting rigidly on a rise in the ground, yards ahead of them. Fortunately, Marakorpa, who had come along, was lagging behind and was thus not present to scare the long-eared animal away. Hence it was an easy target.

Slowly and quietly, Yurgama took his boomerang from his belt, took careful aim and threw it. Before the implement returned to him, the sharp steel cut into the rabbit's neck and killed it.

Fedor and Yurgama went forward talking about taking the animal back to Oenone, skinning and cooking it as an extra part of their picnic. But Marakorpa appeared out of nowhere and had other ideas. He quickly caught the rabbit in his mouth and decided it was going to be his meal.

When the two men returned to the picnic spot, Oenone was not to be seen. At first, Fedor was not concerned. His wife could have been just away temporarily doing something. But just as he was about to call her, he saw a woman's body lying near the billabong.

"Yurgama! Oenone—she's over there!" he said alarmed. The Trooper put a firm restraining hand on his friend.

"Don't move, Fedor," advised the Aborigine. "There's a brown snake near her."

"Oh, no!" cried his companion.

"Try to keep calm," said the Trooper, who felt just as anxious as his friend, but concealed his feeling as best as he could. Nervously, he held his boomerang waiting and hoping for the serpent to lift its head. The minutes seemed like hours as the reptile wriggled its six and a half foot long body closer to Oenone's body.

Fedor broke the silence, "I can't stand it, Yur."

To the Trooper's dismay, the snake heard his voice. But the serpent did what the Aborigine hoped it would do. It lifted its head high in apparent curiosity, long enough for him to throw his weapon at it.

The friends felt relieved when the steel in the implement, cut the reptile's head off.

But the relief was short-lived. Another brown snake, which wasn't as long as the first one, slithered into view near Oenone's body. There must have been a family of them.

When his boomerang returned to him, Yurgama despairingly threw the implement again at the second serpent.

But his weapon missed the reptile. Fedor covered his face in his hands.

However, the agonised feeling of the men that Oenone would be bitten by the snake ended. A kookaburra, possibly one of the two they saw earlier in the red gum, swooped down and caught the serpent in its beak. Yurgama nudged his friend to look and they saw the bird fly high in the sky and drop the snake to the ground, to its death.

Fedor anxiously fussed over Oenone. To his relief, she revived and incoherently muttered that, from what she could remember, she was going to the billabong to fetch some water and blacked out.

"It looks as though she could have just fainted in the hot sun," guessed Yurgama.

"I'll never forget this outing," remarked Fedor kissing Oenone on her forehead. "My beautiful wife could have been taken from me three times in the one day."

The conversation was distracted by the sound of gnawing. The three people looked to see where it came from. In a bush near the party's picnic spot, Marakorpa was thoroughly enjoying himself eating the rabbit.

"We could have all died from spider or snake bites. But while Korpa had that bunny, I don't think he would have paid any attention," joked Oenone.

Danger in the Ocean

Due to a coincidentally large number of deaths in, and resignations from, the Victorian Colonial Police Force, some temporary transfers were made.

Among them was Yurgama's change from his regular post in Tilabrook to St Kilda in Melbourne. Here he was to act as assistant to a veteran upholder of the law, Trooper Rex Maher.

On a quiet Tuesday afternoon, Rex's ten-year-old son Vincent was spending a few hours fishing on the end of the St Kilda beach pier. Marakorpa was with the boy, and the animal dozed the time away while the lad waited patiently, but unsuccessfully, for a bite on his line.

Conditions in St Kilda on the day were peaceful and trouble free. Rex Maher and his black assistant were chatting on the beach to Albert Cathew, an elderly man who hired out boats to the public. He offered the two Troopers the free use of a small boat with paddles, suggesting they take a short jaunt on the ocean. The lawmen could not resist the invitation.

As they paddled out to the end of the pier, with the intention of giving young Vincent a surprise, a change in the weather came over and it got windy. But when the Troopers got closer to where the boy was squatted, it was he who gave them a surprise. The lad was holding on determinedly to his fishing rod which was very bent with a taut line.

"Dad! I've got a bite, a whopper," he yelled to his father.

"He's contending with a big yellow tail kingfish. It could weigh seventy or eighty pounds from what I can see," remarked Yurgama to the boy's father.

"And he is just sitting on the edge of the pier. A fish like that could pull him in," replied Rex. "Vin, let it go. You could be pulled into the water," he advised out loud to his son.

"No, Dad! I can get him," replied the determined lad.

By this time, Marakorpa too had become excited and was running about the pier exuberantly.

At Rex Maher's request, Yurgama threw his boomerang at the boy's taut fishing line. The steel cut the line in half.

But just as the implement returned to land in the boat, Marakorpa slipped from the pier into the ocean.

The two Troopers paddled the boat furiously toward the struggling animal.

"Hang on, Boy!" called the Aborigine fretfully to his pet.

Out of breath, the men reached the weak, exhausted dingo. Rex, who was closer, started to try and lift the animal into the boat, when his son yelled "Yurgama! there's a shark!"

Frighteningly, the boy was right. There was a hammerhead shark swiftly moving near the surface of the water towards Marakorpa.

The Aborigine grabbed his steel-rimmed boomerang and frantically struck at the savage of the sea.

Although he was uncertain whether he caused any wound to the hammerhead, his action succeeded in warding it away into another direction from its pursuit of Marakorpa.

The wind blew stronger and stronger as Rex Maher finally got the dingo into the boat. But as he did so, he accidentally knocked one of the paddles into the sea. In the turmoil, the implement had been left half overlapping the front of the vessel.

With only one paddle, it would have been extremely difficult for the tired Troopers to get to shore. There happened to be rope in the bottom of the boat. Wistfully, Rex Maher wished they could lasso the rope to the pier, before the wind took the vessel away from it.

"Rex, you've given me an idea," said Yurgama.

The Aborigine tied a tight knot around his boomerang with the rope. With all his strength, he threw the curved implement as hard as he could at a pylon of the pier. As he had hoped, the steel wedged deeply into the wood of the pylon.

"Come on, mate, pull! It's our only chance," said the black Trooper, grabbing the rope they still had left, to indicate to his fellow lawman what he meant.

The Aborigine's implement stayed true as the men gradually pulled the boat up against the pier.

With realisation of the serious situation, young Vincent had hurried to get Albert Cathew's help.

Alone in a large row boat, the elderly boatman went out to the worn out Troopers and dingo and slowly but surely, brought them back to shore and safety.

Later, at the St. Kilda Police Station, an old blanket was laid out on the floor for Marakorpa. The dingo lay listless, and to the Aborigine's concern, the animal was not interested in any food or drink offered to him.

"Yurgama, you had better have some food yourself, mate," suggested Rex understandingly, when night fell and the black Trooper had not eaten.

"What have you got?" asked the Aborigine gratefully, but disinterestedly,

"I cooked some bacon and scrambled eggs on toast for you,"

informed his fellow lawman.

Yurgama responded to his colleague's trouble. The plate of food had been put on a table in the same room where Marakorpa rested, and the Aborigine got up to go there. However, when he entered the room, the dingo had his front paw up on the table and was devouring the bacon and eggs. It was a welcome sight for his master. At any other time, he would have rebuked the animal for such an action. But after its unpleasant experience in the day, the Aborigine could only pat his pet approvingly.

Yurgama called his fellow Trooper. When Rex Maher learnt what the dingo had done, he remarked, "with Alby Cathew's help, it looks as though Korpa is back to his villainous, energetic self again."

Thank you, Saint David

On a Christmas Eve afternoon, young Neville Flattery walked into Tilabrook's sandstone Police Station to see Yurgama. The reason for the boy's visit was on behalf of his parents, to extend an invitation to the black Trooper to come to their home that night.

Yurgama was pleased to accept, and when Neville was about to leave, he urged him to stay and talk for a while.

The lad related that he would be serving as altar boy to Father Patrick Maguire, when the priest would be saying midnight Mass that evening. Due to the difficulty of travel over long distances to the various districts, Fr Maguire could only say Mass at Tilabrook, once every four weeks. Mass was celebrated in the Anglican church. The Church of England Minister, the Reverend Thomas Chopadick, was only too pleased to make it available to the Catholics till Fr Maguire's dream to serve his Tilabrook congregation in their own church was hopefully fulfilled.

To attempt to gain the best relief from the searing summer heat, Marakorpa had stretched himself out on the Station floor near a wall. The dingo thumped his bushy tail on the floor when Neville Flattery went over to pat and speak to him. The boy asked the Aborigine why Marakorpa never barked, to which Yurgama said that apparently the dingo was a breed that couldn't bark.

The Trooper nonchalantly inquired after Neville's parents, and to his surprise, the boy said that they bickered constantly. The lad related that his parents' courtship days were spent in Wales. And he was so worried about the present state of their marriage, that he prayed to Saint David, the patron of Wales, to restore the happy relationship his parents enjoyed in their engagement period.

"Dad is making a surprise for me for Christmas, Yurgama. But the best thing I could get for Christmas is for he and Mum to live together happily," declared Neville.

That evening, when the Trooper fulfilled the Flattery's invitation, he was to find out that the boy's worries had foundation.

In the backyard of their home, Druce Flattery, a clerk at the local Magpie Hotel, had set up three chairs and a table with a lighted candle on it.

"What in heaven's name are you doing, Druce?" demanded his tiny wife Thisbe, as her husband sat down and opened a packet of cards on the table.

"I thought when Yurgama comes, the three of us could have a game of cards," explained Druce.

"What, out here? You're getting a bit eccentric aren't you."

"Well it's such a warm night, Dear."

"Looks to me to be preparations for romance in the moonlight," remarked Thisbe sarcastically.

"It's a pity you weren't more romantic," stated her husband critically.

"Druce, this idea is utterly stupid. Take the table and chairs back inside," ordered the woman.

"I'm not going to take this day in day out treatment that you give me, any longer. You need a good spanking, my Dear and I'm going to give it to you," declared Druce.

"You wouldn't dare!" challenged his tiny wife.

"Oh, yes I would," he affirmed.

In the next moments, he picked a twig up off the ground and put his wife over his knee with his foot resting on one of the chairs.

"Put me down this instant, Druce," demanded an indignant Thisbe.

Without making his presence known to the Flattery's, Yurgama had arrived. He stood silent and embarrassed at the gate to their backyard.

However, before Druce could lay the twig to his wife's posterior, the Aborigine whipped his steel-rimmed implement from his belt and threw it. Before returning to the Trooper's feet, the boomerang cut the twig in half near the hotel clerk's hand.

With surprise and discomfort, Druce released his wife. But she did not feel discomfort. She was furious.

"I'll teach you to try and humiliate me in front of outsiders, Druce Flattery," she said angrily.

To her husband's dismay, the woman grabbed some of the cards on the table with the intention of burning them over the candle flame.

"Thisbe! That deck was a gift from my late mother," he cried with anguish.

But before the cards could catch alight on the candle flame, Yurgama threw his boomerang again. Before returning to him the implement cut the top part of the candle off.

"I apologise for my wife's unseemly conduct, Yurgama," said Druce.

"And I apologise for my husband's unseemly conduct, Yurgama," put in Thisbe.

"There has been enough embarrassment, Thisbe. I hope you will now do something constructive and go and make a pot of tea," suggested the hotel clerk.

"Don't try and say you weren't at fault," snapped his wife, leaving to carry out the suggestion.

While she was away, Yurgama tried to make light of the incident. Druce told him that Neville was away helping to clean the church for midnight Mass. This led the boy's father to enthusiastically tell the Trooper that he had made his son a bow and arrows for Christmas.

Yurgama then reiterated to the hotel clerk, the wish of his son in the afternoon, that the best gift his parents could give him for the festive season, would be for them to live together happily.

Later, after the black Trooper parted company with his hosts, Druce told his wife what their son had mentioned to the Aborigine.

"Druce, I've been foolish to you for too long and it has caused our Neville to worry," remarked Thisbe.

"We have both been foolish, Dear," replied her husband.

"Let's fulfil our son's wish," she suggested with a smile and the couple immediately hugged and held each other tightly.

A month later, Neville Flattery called into the Tilabrook Police Station.

"Yurgama, there has been a remarkable change in Mum and Dad's marriage. They can't do enough for each other," he told the Trooper excitedly.

"On Christmas Eve, I told Dad the best gift he and your mother could give you, Neville. I don't know whether that could have caused any change," commented the Aborigine.

"Well, before I get into bed tonight, I must kneel down and formally say thank you, Saint David. It just goes to show that if you pray hard enough and long enough, your prayers will be answered," surmised the boy.

Rescue at Wenchou

The gold discoveries in Australia during the 1850s brought many Chinese to the British Colonies. Among them was Jan Ipp, who came with his two brothers.

Jan's brothers returned to China, but he stayed on after marrying the daughter of an Irish free settler. The Chinaman and his wife Davina bought thirty acres of land in the Tilabrook district. Here they cultivated the land into a market garden to grow vegetables commercially and they called their home "Wenchou" after Jan's birthplace in China.

After they married, the Ipps adopted Shamus a little deaf boy.

It was a warm, sunny Saturday in spring. Jan and Davina had Yurgama as their guest for dinner. While he was carving some tender roast lamb, Jan remarked to Yurgama that the mice population had been in abundance around his home. To eradicate the rodents, he sprinkled a poisonous powder over hunks of cheese. Then he put the cheese on saucers and placed them in various spots.

Davina, who was serving up vegetables, asked her husband where their son was. Immediately, the Aborigine offered to get the lad for dinner and he went outside to look for him.

While their guest was away, Jan put a suggestion to his wife that he had never made before. It surprised her very much. He wanted them to go to China to live and be closer to his family.

Davina reacted with gentle opposition. However, when she saw that the idea meant a lot to her husband, she promised him she would think about it.

Meanwhile, Yurgama came to find Shamus near a shed adjoining the Ipp's home. To the black Trooper's shock, the boy, who didn't see him, was picking up a hunk of the cheese with the poisonous powder sprinkled over it. The Aborigine was about twenty feet away from the child. But when he put the large piece of cheese up to his mouth to take a bite, Yurgama whipped his boomerang from his belt and threw it. Shamus jumped with surprise when the steel sliced off the top part of the cheese he held.

As soon as his boomerang returned to his feet, the Aborigine explained by sign language to the boy the danger of eating the cheese. He then took the lad by the hand into the house.

After dinner, Jan, Shamus and Yurgama went for a long walk over the countryside beyond the market gardener's land. Marakorpa came too and the docile animal did not seem bothered by the occasional attempts of Shamus to get on his back.

The party ambled for about a mile through open country with scattered red stringy bark gums. Then they decided to return home. Just as they were about to turn back, Yurgama saw something out of the corner of his eye. It was a black crow which appeared to be swooping down on something on the ground about fifty yards away. With all his might, the Trooper threw his steel-rimmed boomerang and, in its flight before returning to the Aborigine, the implement struck and killed the crow.

The party discovered the birds would-be victim to be a young kangaroo which had one of its feet caught between two rocks in a bushy glade. It would have been probable that the animal would have had its eyes plucked out by the crow.

Jan and Yurgama carried the kangaroo back to his home and put it in his shed.

When the Aborigine decided to depart from his hosts, the sky was very grey and threatening. However, despite the Ipp's good-willed invitation to him to stay with them overnight, the Trooper considered he could reach Tilabrook on his horse, before any storm broke loose.

But the Aborigine had only ridden a quarter of a mile when loud thunder clapped in the sky. Before Yurgama could urge his chestnut hack into a gallop, a bolt of lightning struck a tree just ahead of them. The stallion reared up with fright causing the Trooper to fall off.

Yurgama was not concussed. But he had a bruised hip and he discovered when he tried to get up that he couldn't walk. He considered he must have broken his ankle. Hence helpless, he lay on the ground as drenching rain poured. He whistled to his horse without luck. It could have galloped for miles, he thought. In the meantime, with a puzzled look on his face, Marakorpa stayed by his master.

In very little time however, help unexpectedly came to the Aborigine. It was Jan coming along the track in his gig. As he assisted Yurgama into the gig, the market gardener told the Aborigine his chestnut had come back to "Wenchou". Thus he knew the Trooper must have been in trouble.

Later in the evening at the Ipp's home, Davina delighted her husband by saying she had given much thought to his desire to return to China. She told him that if he was not happy in Australia, she couldn't be either. Hence, she was very willing for them to leave.

Jan reacted with a broad smile. He remarked, "in the meantime, before we travel, our immediate task is to nurse Yurgama and nurture a young kangaroo."

The World Needs Workers

On flat plains north-west of Tilabrook, lay the Broven merino sheep grazing property.

The property was maintained by Eleanor Broven, a young woman whose mother had died when her daughter was a small child. Eleanor's father had passed on more recently, leaving her with the responsibility of the family estate.

From Wangaratta, the young woman's teenage cousins, Cynthia, Muriel and Susan Broven, came to give temporary companionship and help in running the property, till Eleanor made definite plans for the future.

In this unusual situation, where there was no male to assist on the property, the three Broven girls, under cousin Eleanor's leadership, became sturdy, reliable workers.

On an October morning, a young sinewy, lanky man knocked at the door of the Broven weatherboard house.

Eleanor went to answer the visitor and he was immediately attracted by her handsome, well-built appearance.

"Good morning, Madam. My name is Graham Tash. Trooper Yurgama Jacobs recommended that I come here. He said you might be able to do with a man," announced the fellow.

"What for?" asked Eleanor suspiciously.

"To work," he said.

"Oh well, that's different," she accepted.

"I have a note from Yurgama."

Eleanor quickly read the paper handed to her and asked, "What do you do?"

"I've done plenty of shearing. Your sheep look ready to be clipped," commented the fellow.

The young lady pondered undecided.

"I need a job. I'm almost down to my last penny," he appealed.

"All right!" she agreed. "You can unsaddle your hack in the stable. There's a spare bedroom you can have. Do you agree to wages according to your worth?"

"Yes. I'm sure you will be fair."

Within a few days, the work chores of the Broven females had been noticeably lightened by the arrival of Graham Tash. Cynthia, Muriel and Susan had noticed a change in cousin Eleanor too, with the presence of the young man. The eldest of the three girls, who was starting to fill out into womanhood herself, Cynthia, jokingly warned Tash that the girls felt their cousin had a romantic leaning towards him.

The lanky fellow was to find out that the opinion was true. One mild night, when everyone in the Broven household had supposedly gone to bed, Graham Tash was disturbed. He thought there must have been a prowler and, considering it his duty to be the protector of the maiden-folk, he went out to investigate.

Standing wistfully on the house verandah, silently hoping he would join her, was the curvaceous figure of Eleanor.

Graham declared his surprise, to which she dreamily remarked how beautiful the full moon was. He advised that she ought to go to bed, since it was her turn to milk the family's Jersey cow in the morning. Eleanor commented that it was restful to survey the moonlit scene and listen to the crickets. She asked him to stay with her for a while.

The lanky fellow walked over to her. Her heart beat faster. She hoped he would take her in his arms and draw her lips to his.

Instead, Tash grasped the opportunity to use the woman's mood for other purposes. He told her he was badly in need of a new pair of trousers. Could she give him money in advance to buy some at Tilabrook in the morning.

Disappointed, Eleanor gave her consent, and, with a sly grin, Graham Tash went back to bed.

It was in the afternoon of the following day, that the lanky fellow eventually returned from Tilabrook. Instead of buying trousers, he spent time at the Magpie Hotel and brought back a bottle of Johnnie Walker whisky. Like a naughty boy, he tried to hide the liquor, but Cynthia, Muriel and Susan saw it.

"Graham, you were supposed to be back by mid-day," reminded Muriel.

"Don't you tell your cousin about this whisky will you, girls," he requested.

"What's it worth?" bargained young Susan.

"Susan!" admonished Cynthia.

"I'll give you each a farthing to buy toffee on the next occasion you go to Tilabrook," quickly offered Tash.

"We'll take it," answered Susan,

The other girls were at first undecided about the righteousness of such diplomacy. But the temptation of getting sweet toffee, caused them to relent.

While this exchange was taking place between Tash and the Broven girls in the stable, Yurgama unobtrusively arrived on his stallion with Marakorpa. As his animals drank at a water trough, the Aborigine heard the noise of talk from the stable and went there.

By now, Graham Tash was attempting to get one of the girls to clean the shearing shed for him. They were insisting it was his job.

He made a proposal that they draw straws and the person who picked the shortest, cleaned out the shed. The girls agreed.

Without announcing his presence, Yurgama stood about forty feet away. The lanky fellow picked up four straws of varying lengths from the ground and asked the lasses to take one from his out-stretched hand.

"So that there will be no cheating, we will all close our eyes," he said to the girls.

However, the black Trooper observed that Tash held the longest of the four straws firmly. Hence, when the Brovens had drawn the other, looser, shorter ones, the Aborigine whipped his steel-rimmed boomerang from his belt and threw it. In its transit, the implement cut the last remaining straw in half above where the fellow held it in his hand.

Yurgama managed to get his returned boomerang back inside his belt before Tash said everyone could open their eyes.

"You have to clean the shed, Graham," concluded Muriel when the straws were examined for their lengths. The lanky fellow scratched his curly black hair with puzzlement.

The Aborigine, announcing himself, said with innocence, "What? Did you get the shortest straw, Graham?"

"Hello, Yur. What are you doing here?" asked Tash.

The Trooper told him he came to see if Eleanor gave him a job. With gratitude, the fellow told Yurgama that he was liking his new employment.

The Broven girls wanted the Aborigine to show them how to throw his boomerang. Tash, in the meantime, went to carry out his shed cleaning chore.

Each time the girls threw Yurgama's implement, it never returned to them. The Aborigine employed Marakorpa to fetch back the curved piece of wood. Upon previous training, the dingo picked the boomerang up in his mouth from the outside, so that he did not cut his mouth on the steel on the inside.

After enjoying a cup of hot Broven tea, Yurgama was about to make his departure. But Susan, the last to play with his boomerang, announced that she could not find it. Eventually, the Aborigine decided to leave without his lost implement.

Much later that day, Graham Tash walked into the Broven house and proudly told Eleanor he had sheared the sheep.

"What with? I thought the clippers were broken," said the woman.

"Yurgama's boomerang did the job perfectly," answered the fellow.

Shocked and in disbelief, Eleanor went out and saw that the sheep had been very well shorn.

She felt increased attachment toward Tash.

But her pleased approval of him was short-lived.

When the lanky fellow was supposed to be packing the wool the next day, Eleanor caught him drinking the Johnnie Walker.

"Graham, the world needs workers, the colonies need workers and I don't need a loafer. Pack your belongings and leave immediately," she ordered angrily.

In Tilabrook, a glum Graham Tash went into the Police Station and returned Yurgama's boomerang to him. He was asked by the Trooper if anything was wrong. The lanky fellow related his bad news, remarking that he couldn't blame Eleanor.

While they spoke, the Aborigine happened to notice through a Station window, the very lady in question. She was going along the street in her carriage with a smart green dress on and a yellow bonnet atop her head. She must have been shopping in the town.

The Trooper called Marakorpa and hurried outside with a perplexed Tash following.

The Aborigine threw his boomerang at the moving Broven carriage. As he hoped, the back of the steel-rimmed implement knocked Eleanor's bonnet off her head onto the ground.

As his boomerang returned to him, Yurgama told Marakorpa to fetch the bonnet back to him.

He handed it to the shearer.

"Graham, this will give you a reason to go back to Eleanor and try to win her forgiveness," suggested the Trooper.

When the sun was sinking in the west, Tash nervously knocked at the Broven house.

"I thought I told you to leave here," declared an angry Eleanor when she answered the door.

"Eleanor, I've just come back to return your bonnet," offered the fellow.

"Oh, it must have fallen off in the breeze, in Tilabrook?" asked the young woman.

Tash did not answer. He looked at her appealingly and asked her to give him another chance.

"Oh, I will, Graham," said Eleanor with changed emotions. "I want to belong to you. I want you to be part of this place."

"I want to belong to you too," responded the lanky fellow as she rested her head on his chest and in his arms.

Unknown to the couple, three Broven sisters were listening to the intimate interlude.

"I've got a feeling we might be guests at a wedding," declared Susan to the other two eavesdroppers.

Evergreen

Outside a modest, but pretty, mud brick home in Jessel Parade, Tilabrook, seven-year-old John Hump and his five-year-old sister Sabrina were being seen off to school by their young mother.

In preparation for the coming winter months, she had knitted her children red woollen mittens and matching red woollen scarves. On this fresh May morning, she devotedly put the mittens on their little hands and wove the scarves round their necks. Cheese sandwiches, tomato and onion sandwiches, an apple and orange had been prepared for John and Sabrina. Their mother handed the lunch food to them, and as always, she fondly kissed them goodbye.

John, who had a recent basin haircut, and Sabrina, with sausage curls in her hair, enthusiastically hugged Marakorpa who wanted to go with them.

The dingo was being looked after by the Humps, while Yurgama was away for a week. He had been called upon to act as a guard with other Troopers to a valuable transportation of gold from Heathcote to Melbourne.

The Tilabrook Primary School was also situated in Jessel Parade. It was just a three hundred yard walk past the Town Hall for the Hump children. On each side of the public weatherboard building, tall poplars grew. As autumn always decided, the poplar leaves were turning gold and starting to fall. This fascinated Sabrina, and she dawdled behind John to gaze at the trees. He called to his sister to hurry up, saying they would be late for school.

In the large classroom for the first three grades of Tilabrook district children, Miss Faddin, the teacher, called upon her young students to answer when she called their name from a roll book.

After the conclusion of this daily opening ritual, she opened the day's lessons with arithmetic.

After the pupils' morning playtime break, history followed. The teacher talked about Richard The Lionheart, the crusaders, Oliver Cromwell and other distinguished persons of the mother country lineage.

During this talk to the children, Sabrina put up her hand and said she desperately wanted to go to the toilet.

As a light reprieve from the lessons, Miss Faddin started a discussion on the occupations of her pupils' fathers. Some children mentioned that their father was a farmer, others said he was a Bank manager, a bootmaker, a blacksmith. They all seemed more important jobs than the one his father had, thought John Hump. His father was a janitor who cleaned the Town Hall, the Court House, Police Station and other Tilabrook premises. Hence, the little boy felt ashamed to tell Miss Faddin. The dignified, stiff, but warm teacher noticed John's feelings. She called to his sister to tell him he need not feel ashamed of their father's honourable occupation.

But Sabrina was nowhere in the classroom to be seen and it was half an hour since she had been excused to leave the room.

One little girl who sat next to Sabrina offered information that the sausage curls lass told her she felt like going for a walk in the ironbark bush near the school.

"Oh, if she did that, she could get lost. That bush area is thick," said Miss Faddin with dismay.

"Miss Faddin, I could run home and get Korpa whom we are feeding while Trooper Jacobs is away. The dingo may be able to pick up Sabrina's scent," suggested John.

"Yes, it's worth a try. We must do something. But don't let your mother find out why you have returned, John. We don't want her to worry needlessly. There may not be reason to raise an alarm—I hope," said the woman.

When John returned with Marakorpa, Miss Faddin told the other children they could stay in the classroom and draw, or play outside.

Before venturing into the bush with his teacher and the dingo, John put the scarf his sister left behind, up to the animal's nose. Marakorpa sniffed the scarf, and with coaxing from John, the dingo seemed to understand what was wanted of him.

"Oh, I think we are on a wild goose chase, John. Korpa has his nose to the ground, but the three of us are probably just going for a walk, as far as he is concerned. We may get lost ourselves," declared Miss Faddin after they must have covered a mile through the ironbark.

"Don't worry, Miss Faddin. I know this country like the back of my hand. Sabrina doesn't. But let's persevere. If she did wander off in here, I feel fairly certain Marakorpa knows we want him to find her," urged John.

After another quarter of a mile, the teacher considered it silly to go on and decided to go back. Then Marakorpa discovered a red mitten—Sabrina's mitten.

A horrible feeling gripped Miss Faddin. The dingo was on the little girl's trail, but had she come to harm?

As Marakorpa continued tracking for them, the dark brown

reddish iron bark gums and undergrowth now seemed silently sinister looking to the teacher.

They had not gone much further, even though she felt as if they had, and she was just about to unwisely mutter to the little boy that she felt the worst had befallen his sister. But the monotony of the walking was broken when Marakorpa unexpectedly bounded forward. John hurried to catch up with him.

And moments later, he called back with delight to his not so dignified, panting teacher: "Miss Faddin! Sabrina is here! She's safe!"

The tired woman felt uplifted relief as she soon laid eyes on the little girl with the sausage curls, contentedly eating her lunch food. As if he was aware of the anxiety over her disappearance, Marakorpa too was overjoyed to see her.

"Sabrina! Why didn't you come back into class? Why did you wander off here? If something had happened to you, it would have broken your mother's heart," admonished the youngster's teacher.

"I'm really sorry, Miss Faddin. It looks as though I've caused you awful worry," apologised the girl.

"Yes, I'm afraid you have, dear. Why did you do it?"

"I saw that the leaves on the trees near the Town Hall had changed colour and were starting to fall. I wanted to see if I could find some other trees in the bush, whose leaves changed colour and fell to the ground."

"Australian gum trees never lose their leaves and they never change their colour," informed the teacher.

"Gee, if I'd known that, I wouldn't have come here."

Miss Faddin lifted her eyes in appeal to the heavens. Then, with a forgiving smile, she patted the dingo and said, "Oh well. Thanks to Korpa, we found you."

The Visionary

In the 1840s, a young Scotsman and his newly won bride, visited the United States. The visit was partly of a business purpose and partly to be enjoyed as a honeymoon by the couple. On the business side, the Scotsman was inspecting some cotton plantations in the south which were owned by his wealthy father, who had scattered business interests throughout the new world.

Horrified by the fact that the plantations were run by African slaves, the Scotsman's bride persuaded him to allow the Negroes to go free or remain as free employees. Out of gratitude, one young Negro, Tobias Macember requested and pestered the young couple to let him be their personal servant. Hence, in the years that followed, Toby Macember went back to Scotland with the couple and always remained with them on other travels they made.

In Australia, the Scotsman's father had two large merino sheep studs in one of the colonies. Some twenty years later, after his son and daughter-in-law had made an earlier visit to the land down under with their loyal, devoted Toby, they decided to settle in the land of the kangaroo. The Scot couple's home where they decided to continue to raise their children, lay in the Swan river district in Western Australia.

After the passing of two more years, the Scot decided to speculate the proposition of increasing the family fortune by buying properties in the rich eastern colonies and he sailed for them. But the six month duration of time that he promised his wife he would be away, elapsed. When twelve months passed and he still had not returned, Toby Macember insisted to his distressed Mistress that he should search for his Master. Even though the Scot couple preferred that their Negro servant call them by their first names, he always referred to them as his Mistress and Master.

In his search, Toby not only went to the large colonial ports, he travelled through the inland. Once he stopped over in Tilabrook for a night. Here, he got into deep conversation with a group of five boisterous farmers in the bar of the Magpie Hotel. The men were amused at what the Negro had to say and thought he was crazy.

"You gents may not believe me, but I think mankind is progressing so much that I wouldn't be surprised if the day came when he invented a carriage which didn't need a horse to pull it and a machine that could fly him over the countryside and the sea," he declared to the men sitting with him around a table.

"Next he will be telling us that we will be able to fly to the moon and the stars," remarked one man amidst the mirth.

"Yes," confirmed the unperturbed Negro.

"And I will go further to say that one day we will be able to control the weather and turn all the ice wastes and deserts into rich food producing land."

"This guy is a lunatic! Let's take him outside and examine his head, fellers," suggested one big well-to-do chap with a cigar.

Immediately, his idea was taken up. The farmers put down their beer and whisky glasses, grabbed Toby and carried him outside to a side alleyway. A bartender, concerned for the Negro's safety, was reassured by the men that they would not hurt him.

But in the alleyway, while the other farmers held Toby down, the well-to-do chap raised his cigar above his head, tormenting the Negro with the declaration that he was going to singe his woolly hair.

"Chaps, I think I ought to burn the silly thoughts our friend has in his head."

"Yes, go ahead, Cato," urged the other men.

At the precise moment in which this incident was taking place, Marakorpa was passing the end of the street with his Aboriginal Master sauntering behind. The dingo saw the rumpus going on in the alley. He stood still like a statue as he watched inquisitively. Intuition told Yurgama something was wrong when he saw his pet like this. The Trooper quickened his step and withdrew his boomerang. When he saw the scene the dingo was taking in, he threw his implement. In its flight, it cut Cato's cigar in half.

As the boomerang returned to the black Trooper's feet, the men let go of Toby.

"You ought to be ashamed of yourselves, scaring people," scolded the Aborigine.

"We weren't going to hurt him, Yurgama," said Cato.

"You have told me that before, Cato Brennan. One day you will go too far in ring-leading these incidents," warned the Trooper. "Disperse, go to your families and sober up—the lot of you—for peace sake," he continued.

As the men obeyed the order, Brennan brushed passed the lawman angrily. He did not like Yurgama singling him out.

"Are you all right, mate?" asked the Aborigine of the Negro.

"Yes, I'm okay. I can tell you, I was a bit scared though."

"I know those chaps. I don't think they would have harmed you," reassured the Trooper.

"They sure had me fooled," commented Toby.

The two blacks introduced each other and the Negro mentioned why he was passing through Tilabrook. When the Aborigine confirmed to him that his Scottish benefactor had not been seen in the district, Toby said he would leave on the stagecoach the following morning after staying overnight at the hotel.

But about an hour later, when the Negro was taking a sight-seeing stroll around the town to fill in time, he passed the Police Station and noticed through the window Cato Brennan with a rifle. Toby was going to continue his walk, till it instantly occurred to him that Brennan seemed to be pointing the gun at someone. He crept back to the Station and quietly pushed the half-ajar front doors. Cato had the firearm trained on Yurgama, and fortunately, the big farmer had his back to the Station's entrance.

"You must think you're a big man, Yurgama—dishing out orders to people having some harmless fun," declared Brennan in scathing tones.

"You're more under the weather now than you were then, Cato. Lower your rifle and walk out of here and I won't make any charge against you," offered the Aborigine seeing Toby entering softly.

"You must be joking if you think I would surrender the upper hand that I have. I intend teaching you a lesson, Yurgama. Now it's me whose giving the orders. Get into one of those cells," threatened Brennan.

The Trooper stood his ground silently as Toby crept slowly

up to the big farmer. The order to the Aborigine to get into the cell was repeated and still it went unheeded. Tension mounted.

"I'll give you one last chance, Yurgama," warned Brennan cocking the rifle. Again his words went unheeded. Angrily impatient, the farmer was about to pull the rifle trigger. But Toby, who was right behind him now, caught him in a suffocating bear hug which forced him to drop the gun.

The following morning, as the coach was about to leave Tilabrook with the Negro on it, the Aborigine shook hands with him.

"Pleased to have met you, Toby. You passed by at the right moment to save me from serious injury or possibly being killed."

"And you passed by at the right moment to save me, Yurgama," added the Negro to the Aborigine's grateful remark. "What breed is your dog?" he said changing onto a lighter subject.

"He's a dingo. There is a theory that when the Aborigines first came to Australia, they brought the dingo with them."

"Do they only have three legs?" asked Toby hesitantly, considering his question may have been silly.

"No, they have four legs," began Yurgama and he briefly related the history of how Marakorpa had to lose his front left leg.

Departure time came.

"I hope you find your friend," wished the Trooper.

The Negro waved to him as the coach driver urged his four horse team to move along.

Toby did find his Scottish friend and benefactor. They returned to the Swan river district and the Negro lived to a ripe old age to see one of his visionary thoughts, the horseless carriage, become a reality.

The Lady Bushranger

When the four-horse stage came to a halt outside the Cobb & Co coach depot in Tilabrook, one of the passengers got off hurriedly and went straight to the Police Station.

In his hurry, he nearly tripped over Marakorpa. The dingo was lying flat out on the floor at the Station's entrance, so that he could enjoy the warm sunshine filtering through.

Yurgama, greeted the man with concern, for he was an old friend and he had his arm in a sling.

"Hello, Jim! What brings you to Tilabrook?"

"Yurgama, the Commercial Banking Company of Sydney, Hartog branch was held up this morning by a young couple," announced the man.

"Is that how your arm got hurt?" asked the black Trooper.

"Yes, but nobody else was injured."

"What happened?"

"I was depositing money at the Bank when this girl, accompanied by a young chap, strode in and announced that they were holding up the place. The girl, who was a beautiful looking kid, did all the directing. She told the teller if he didn't empty the safe, I would get killed. The teller hesitated, hoping she was bluffing. But she brandished a knife and unexpectedly slashed my arm with it to show she meant business.

"How's your arm now?" asked Yurgama with sympathy.

"It's still pretty sore. But Doc Wudder happened to be in

Hartog and I was able to get him to attend to it.

"This lass and her crony can't be left on the loose. She sounds dangerous. I'll get details, descriptions from you, Jim and then try to track the couple down," said the Aborigine.

Meanwhile, in thick bushland halfway between the town of Hartog and Tilabrook, Artemas Evans and Powell Cullen were near a camp fire counting the money they had successfully robbed from the Bank. Powell Cullen was a tall, thin, gangly man with a weak, submissive character. Artemas Evans was a shapely brunette with a pretty face that contrasted sharply with her forceful disposition. She seemed as innocent as an angel in appearance, but dressed and behaved like a man.

"I make it to be 3,000 quid, Art. What a haul! This could set us up for life, Darling," declared a delighted Powell as he put the money away.

"Don't call me Darling," said Artemas irately, getting up.

"Art, we could settle down with this cash. We wouldn't have to pull any more jobs," said the young man.

"What do you mean, we?" demanded the girl, pacing around moodily.

"You know how I feel about you. You're the only person who makes my life worthwhile."

"Don't start that again. I can't stand men getting sentimental with me—most of all you."

"But you mean so much to me. We could be so happy together," appealed Cullen with tears in his eyes. "You, me and the money—that's all that matters to me," he continued.

"What makes you think you're going to get some of the money?" asked Artemas with an ugly smile coming over her face.

"I had no doubt," commenced Cullen feeling uncomfortable.

His discomfort was justified. In the next moment, Miss Evans took out her knife and aimed it at him.

"Art, what are you doing?" cried the man, shuffling about. He spoke no more. The girl threw the knife and it entered his chest near the heart. Ruthlessly, she pulled it out of his chest.

As her partner lay dying and looking at her with a hopeless, glazed expression in his eyes, the young lady took the money and climbed a tree. It was a very thick box gum without any low branches. But she went up it like a Pacific Islander goes up a coconut palm. Between two high forked branches, she planted the bag of legal tender.

Not feeling like spending the evening in the place, Artemas Evans gave the agonised, prostrate Cullen a disdainful look and decided she would go to Tilabrook and have a good time at the hotel. Her intention was to return to collect the money and leave the district the following morning.

By mid-afternoon, the attractive Miss Evans was seen on her black gelding as it paced down Jessel Parade. She tethered her horse outside the Magpie Hotel.

Half an hour later, she was quite under the influence of heavy indulgence in whisky. She commenced tormenting a blind boy, who, with his mother, was waiting for his father in the hotel foyer. The family was also only staying overnight in the town. In their case, it was for business reasons.

An elderly bartender, as well as the mother, repeatedly appealed to the girl to leave the lad alone. But she was too drunk. The bartender warned that he would get the Trooper. But Miss Evans persisted. Thus he felt obliged to carry out his threat.

While he was away getting Yurgama, Artemas ordered the frightened boy to get the Aborigine, himself.

"That old fool thinks a Trooper with a silly arkana would worry me. I'll show him. You get him for me kid!"

"But I can't see, Madam," pleaded the lad. "Nonsense! You're only imagining things. Now do as I say or I'll pour this grog over your head. I'll give you to the count of ten," said the lass.

While the girl counted out this number, the mother of the boy tried to draw him away. But Miss Evans just pushed her onto the floor. She finally declared the double figure and raised a half-full bottle of Johnnie Walker with the intention of tipping it over the boy's head.

But as she was about to do so, the bottle smashed in her hand, without spilling onto the lad.

Yurgama had arrived on the scene and thrown his boomerang which caused the breakage of the bottle. When the implement returned to his feet, he picked it up and put it back inside his belt. Artemas Evans felt humiliated and expressed anger.

"I don't know who you are, young lady. But I think you could do with a good spanking," uttered Yurgama with a smile. He was impressed by the girl's beauty and went forward to arrest her.

To his shock, Artemas made a swing at him with the bottle handle still in her hand. The broken glass missed cutting the Aborigine's face by inches. But as he stepped back to avoid the impact, he lost his footing and fell to the floor. Immediately, Miss Evans took out her knife with the intention of throwing it at the Trooper, like she threw it at Cullen. The mother of the boy screamed. Frantically, Yurgama rolled onto his side, whipped his boomerang from his belt and threw it. The curved implement knocked the knife out of the girl's raised hand.

The Aborigine got up quickly to take the lass into custody. He eventually overcame her. But she proved surprisingly strong and he had difficulty subduing her.

To the end, she refused to cooperate and answer questions. A hunch led Yurgama to call in his friend with the injured arm. He of course exposed Artemas as being part of the Hartog Bank hold up. But still she refused to cooperate.

Weeks later, though, a shepherd reported finding Powell Cullen's corpse and the stolen money.

Yurgama had not bargained for the fact that neither he nor the shepherd would be able to climb the tree to get the cash. Finally an experiment was risked. One end of a length of rope was tied to his boomerang. He then stepped back from the tree and threw the implement as hard as he could near the forked branches where the money lay. As was hoped, the boomerang wedged deep into the wood at right angles, with the lower end of the implement sticking out. The preliminary precaution of swinging on the rope several times was taken. Yurgama at last felt prepared to take the risk and climb the tree with the rope aid and only his wedged weapon to support his weight.

It was a tense interlude, with the shepherd feeling the most worry. But the boomerang stayed true, and Yurgama was able to drop the money to the ground after he reached the forked branches and slither down safely.

The worry of the boomerang being able to hold a man's weight truly proved needless. The two men were unable to free it from the gum after they pulled on the rope many times. However, when the rope was tied to the saddle of the Aborigine's chestnut, the might of the stallion being led away from the tree soon ensured the retrieval of the implement.

"Who would be able to climb a tree like that and put the money there, Yurgama?" asked the shepherd.

"I think I know. But I don't know whether you would believe

me, if I told you," replied the Trooper.

"I think I can guess. It was probably a black tigress named Artemas Evans."

"You're probably correct, from what I've learnt of her."

"I heard about her referring to your steel-rimmed boomerang as a silly arkana. You may as well call it arkana," suggested the shepherd.

"It's certainly a shorter name," agreed the Aborigine.

Expectant Mothers

The four-wheeled, black-hooded phaeton carriage, drawn by two horses, ploughed through the mud of Jessel Parade on a cold winter's day. The only passenger in the phaeton carriage was Sir Martin Vaducon, owner of the Magpie Hotel and the Vaducon Men's Tailors of Tilabrook. Along with these assets, Sir Martin and his wife Lady Winifred lived in a stately quartz rubble residence in the north of the town. The English couple were considered to be Tilabrook's wealthiest citizens.

The Vaducon phaeton was a familiar sight in the district. But the sight of it about to pass the Police Station now caused Yurgama to rush out.

Across the street, Neville Flattery, the young boy, looked ready to pull an arrow from the bow his father gave him for Christmas a year or two before. And he alarmingly appeared as if he was going to fire it at Sir Martin.

But as the lad drew back his bow, Yurgama managed to throw his arkana. It cut the bow string just before the arrow was about to be released.

As soon as he picked up his returned implement. Yurgama went over to the boy.

"Neville, what are you doing?" asked the black Trooper.

"I was going to put an arrow through Sir Martin's top hat and cause him dismayed discomfort," answered the lad angrily.

"Why, has Sir Martin made you angry? He is your father's boss and you could get your Dad in trouble by playing such pranks."

"That's just it, Yurgama. Dad has been dismissed from his job. The Vaducons have a highly bred border collie bitch called Empress. She has been on heat and many of the dogs about town have given her attention—including Marakorpa."

"That wouldn't surprise me," commented the Aborigine phlegmatically, but lightly. "Go on."

"Understandably, the Vaducons don't want Empress to have offspring off any old breed of dog. But she's been carelessly allowed to roam Tilabrook and is now going to have pups. We recently acquired a mongrel called Keenan. Keenan was the only dog Sir Martin saw near Empress and he has admonished Dad for it. Dad tried to explain to him and Sir Martin dismissed him from his position as clerk at the Magpie."

"I'm sure the good knight's action was probably done in the heat of the moment, Neville."

"Well, Mum is expecting a baby soon, Yurgama. And now that Dad is out of a job, you can understand his heavy burden of worry wondering how he is going to support us."

"I'll tell Sir Martin. I'm sure he will change his mind."

"I feel obliged to confess that I've made use of some firecrackers I obtained a long time ago from Mr Ipp, the Chinese market gardener. These firecrackers make a real loud bang," informed the lad.

"Yes," said the Trooper anxiously.

"I went to the Vaducon's residence this morning. I knew there wouldn't be anyone about. Lady Winifred has sailed to London for some months to see old friends, and Sir Martin had called a meeting at the Hotel for all his employees, including his house servants.”

“What did you do?”

“The Vaducon drawing room window had been left ajar. I got in and planted the firecrackers.”

“Where?”

“I put a couple in the fireplace, put one in Sir Martin’s pipe and tied one, where it could not be seen, to an oil lamp on a sideboard.”

“Such pranks would not help your father’s cause, Neville, if Sir Martin found out. I’ll go to his place immediately and try to get hold of those firecrackers before they are lit.”

“Thanks a lot, Yurgama.”

“You didn’t plant crackers anywhere else in the home, did you?”

“No.”

Ten minutes later:—

“Yurgama, how nice to see you. Come on in.”

“Thank you, Sir Martin,” acknowledged the Aborigine to the austere, wealthy Englishman’s invitation. “My visit isn’t a social imposition?”

“You’re welcome here any time, my good fellow. Shortly, I’ll get the maid to bring beverage and cake. In the meantime, I was just about to listen to my butler play some marvellous concertos on the piano. My Winifred may be scatterbrained and extravagant, but I do miss her. Music soothes loneliness, don’t you agree?”

“Yes,” said Yurgama, relieved to see that the fireplace had not been lit yet in the attractive Vaducon drawing room.

“Yurgama, what are you doing,” asked Sir Martin. The Aborigine was rustling through the paper and wood which was ready to burn in the fireplace.

"Oh, nothing," said the Trooper clumsily, as he managed to retrieve the two planted firecrackers without them being seen.

"Here, catch these," said the Englishman throwing an expensive looking two inch long packet of matches to the Aborigine. "You can light that fire while you're there," he suggested to his guest.

An hour passed without incident while the butler played to his employer's joy, and the Aborigine considered it inadvisable to speak.

Then, as the light of the late afternoon gave way to the darkness of night, Sir Martin got up, and took his matches to light the lamp on the sideboard. He struck a match, held it downwards and moved it near the lamp. Yurgama, from his armchair, tossed his arkana. The implement cut the match in half and the flame quickly went out.

"Yurgama! What in heaven's name are you doing?" appealed the Englishman after the arkana came back to land in front of the Trooper's chair.

The Aboriginal guest immediately wanted to tell his host everything.

"Sir Martin, that wasn't a practical joke. You would have been the victim of a greater shock had I not thrown the boomerang," he started.

"Never mind, Yurgama," stopped the Englishman with a wave of his hand. "Our pianist is coming to a pleasing part of an enjoyable rhapsody."

The Trooper was pressed to stay and enjoy a light tea of soup and cheese on toast, around the fire. Not once was he able to give the reason for his visit. Sir Martin talked without ceasing.

"Timms!" he declared to his butler during the meal. "I never realised you are such a fine pianist. Could you play more for me, tonight?"

"You compliment me, Sir," agreed the butler, who was as equally austere as his employer.

Through the lateness of the night, the piano continued to be played by the butler, and Sir Martin clapped and continued to compliment the pieces.

In his armchair, Yurgama inadvertently fell asleep.

It was close to midnight when he was sharply awakened by the striking of another match. Sir Martin was about to light his pipe. Hurriedly and awkwardly, the Aborigine got his arkana from his belt and tossed it again. And again the steel-rimmed implement cut the match held by the Englishman before he lit his pipe and the firecracker hidden inside.

"Yurgama! I acknowledge your accuracy," began Sir Martin rather angrily. "That is the second time you have carried out that joke. Don't you think it's a bit stale. I hope, too, that you don't sometimes forget that your arkana is a lethal weapon."

Yurgama, pleased, picked up his returned implement. At last he had gotten a chance of a hearing with his wealthy host. And he told him everything.

"That scallywag young Neville must have been really angry with me to dangerously want to fire an arrow and plant firecrackers here. He must love his father," commented Sir Martin.

Without contemplation, the Englishman told the Aborigine, he would immediately reinstate Druce Flattery to his former job at the hotel.

The litter of seven pups which Empress gave birth to turned out to be a cross between border collie and dingo. It meant only one conclusion could be drawn: Marakorpa was the father.

And Mrs Thisbe Flattery gave birth to a healthy seven

pound baby girl. Neville's good regard for Sir Martin had been restored. But the boy came to like the Englishman more. He raised Druce Flattery's wages after learning of the new arrival to their family.

An Answered Prayer

Port Arthur, the convict settlement off Van Diemen's Land, included men who were not really criminal types.

One such man was Stanley Udford who was sentenced at the Old Bailey in London to transportation to the colonies for seven years. Stan Udford's crime was that he was unable to completely pay for the medical treatment for his seriously ill father-in-law.

Like other convicts, he endured the hard times of a tedious, long journey, stern treatment and other discomforts, like the allowance of only one pint of water a day per person.

Once in Van Diemen's Land, Stan received lashes to his back on a trumped up charge of insubordination.

But young Udford's spirit remained undaunted and he always retained an extraordinary compassion for those who harmed him.

His luck changed. He won a ticket of leave, became a free man and went to mainland Australia.

In Tilabrook, Stan saved enough money to buy a poultry farm. And it was here that he was to remain for the rest of his days.

He never returned to England. But all through his life, he carried the prayer and dream that he would see his beloved wife Isobel again.

In his elder years, the good health of the happy Stan Udford suddenly deteriorated.

The event took place when, for no apparent reason, he fell from the back of the only companion he could call his own—his 23-year-old mare Quenby.

When Stan regained consciousness, Quenby was nuzzling at his hair. The man struggled to his feet, put his arms around the horse's neck and, with coaxing, the mare intelligently carted him back to his house.

With neighbours' help fortunately coming in the emergency, Eric Wudder was called. The physician predicted that the respected poultry farmer may not have long to live. He ordered Stan to take more daily rest if he was to have any hope of recovery.

Each morning from then on, Yurgama made time to go to the Udford farm, feed the poultry, collect the eggs, clean up and do other chores.

At the break of day, the Aborigine would go through the poultry sheds where the fowls slept on perches which hung from the roofs on thick string.

On one occasion, Marakorpa followed his Master in. One sleeping hen captivated the animal. With a villainous look in his eyes, it was obvious that he was going to spring at the bird. Yurgama, who was about twenty yards away, ordered his pet away. However, Marakorpa ignored him.

But just before the dingo was able to jump up at the fowl, the Aborigine whipped his arkana from his belt and threw it. The steel-rimmed implement snapped the string holding up one end of the perch.

The hen squawked and fluttered to the ground, with the three-legged animal after it.

When his arkana returned to him, the Aborigine picked it up quickly and dashed after the dingo.

With the flat part of his implement he hit his pet hard on the back.

The blow was effective. Marakorpa never chased fowls again.

One morning, the black Trooper joined Stan Udford for breakfast.

"Yurgama," he began. "If I'm to leave this life soon, as Doc Wudder thinks I may, I want to bequeath this place to you."

"No, you mustn't," reacted the Aborigine, overwhelmed and embarrassed.

"No argument, mate. I insist. I've already made out my will."

Yurgama was dumbfounded.

"Here, get me a knife so I can cut the cap off this boiled egg," instructed Stan.

When the Aborigine went to get the knife, the old man stopped him saying, "No, on second thought, you can give me your arkana." And he cut his egg with the curved implement.

"Stan, if you do die, is there anything you want done?" offered the Trooper inadequately.

"Now that you mention it, Yurgama, I would be grateful if you could make sure Quenby is looked after."

"That's the least I can do," agreed the Aborigine instantly.

"You have already done a lot for me, Yur," added the poultry farmer emphatically.

Then, on the only day the Aborigine did not go to the poultry farm, it happened: Stan Udford passed away.

Time marched on into the afternoon and the old man still had not left his bed. Mrs Mary Hump, the wife of janitor John Hump who cleaned the Tilabrook Police Station and other public premises, found Stan. She had gone to the Udford farm to buy eggs.

Considering that something maybe wrong, she went into the house.

"Mr Udford, are you all right?" she asked when she saw him in bed.

The poultry farmer did not say anything immediately. He just gazed at her. His eyes looked delirious.

"Isobel!" he at last started. "I can't believe it's really you. Come and sit on the bed. Let me hold your hand, so that I know I'm not dreaming."

Mary Hump was hesitant.

"Come near me, my Darling," muttered on the old man. "You're just as I remember you. No different to what you were on the day we married."

With kind realisation that this lonely man was dying, the young woman went straight to his side.

At first, he held her hand strongly and enthusiastically. But his hold became limp. He was weakening fast.

"My dream has come true, Isobel. It's so wonderful to see you again," he gasped, almost inaudible.

Mary Hump was about to speak, when he gasped again.

"Dear, heat me a cup of warm milk, the way you used to."

He tried to keep speaking, but the words did not come out. The young woman looked at him, uncertain what to do. And after a last desperate attempt to keep breathing, Stanley Udford's body became still.

Mary Hump went to get Doctor Wudder and the Reverend Chopadick. When she told Yurgama about her presence with Stan Udford in his last moments, the Aborigine was emotionally moved with a mixture of sadness and joy for the poultry farmer.

"Mrs Hump, you showed wonderfully kind initiative," he
declared gratefully to the janitor's wife.

Quenby lived on till she was twenty-eight. The placid mare
spent these last years peacefully and contentedly in a rich
grassy paddock. It was situated at the back of the Hump's
home and owned by them.

Lawmen Hater

Over dry, grassy, hilly countryside in the Tilabrook district, Yurgama rode on his chestnut stallion at a dawdled pace, with Marakorpa romping energetically ahead of the horse.

Atop a high hill, the Aborigine briefly rested his stallion and surveyed the panorama. To his left, in a valley below, there commenced an area of grey box gum bushland. From here, a horseman came cantering towards Yurgama.

"Trooper!" he yelled. "My friend back in the bush has taken a nasty fall from his horse. Could you help us out?"

"Yes, certainly!" yelled back Yurgama. And he urged his stallion forward.

But the black Trooper was deceived. Two friends of the man were in the bush and neither of them was in trouble. Yurgama recognised one of them.

"Boar roar. I presume you escaped from Pentridge again and these two cohorts aided you."

"Such an intelligently correct assumption, Jacobs," confirmed Robin "Boar roar" Chakley. He was a big man who acquired his nickname because of his loud tongue and desire to assume leadership of his criminal friends. He had served two terms in Pentridge Prison, Melbourne. When he escaped the first time, Yurgama became partially responsible for his recapture.

"Get down from the horse," ordered the big escapee in a changed serious, menacing tone.

Tauntingly, Yurgama stayed where he was.

"Do as Boar says," added one of the other men.

Unexpectedly, he grabbed the Aborigine's leg from out of his stirrup and yanked it.

Fortunately, in his forced drop to the ground, Yurgama managed not to hurt himself.

"Good work, Col," commended Boar roar to his friend. "Take him under control, before he tries anything," instructed the escapee.

With the assistance of the third member of the trio, Yurgama had his arms painfully twisted.

"I'll just take this arkana of yours, Jacobs," said Boar roar pulling the Aborigine's implement from his belt.

The escapee spoke sarcastically: "You helped bring about my recapture into prison. But don't think I want revenge. I know you were only doing your job. But you see, Jacobs, you're part of a profession that displeases me. And sadly you're going to have to be punished. It's nothing personal though remember."

"Are we going to have some fun with him, Boar?" gleefully asked the man called Col.

Marakorpa sauntered in upon the scene and he went up to the big escapee who whistled him.

"It's the Trooper's dog," informed Col.

"A nice dog too," commented the escapee patting the friendly dingo.

"Funny how he has only got three legs," added the other man—a pot-bellied fellow. He and Col had thankfully eased their hold on the Aborigine.

"It would be a shame if I had to cut the dog's other front leg off with Jacob's arkana, Ben," replied the escapee to that pot-bellied chap.

"He wouldn't be able to walk then," put in Col. The three men laughed at the dismayed Trooper.

"Take it out on me. But don't harm the dingo. He hasn't hurt you," appealed the Aborigine.

Boar roar burrowed into some possessions and pulled out a huge pear.

"All right Jacobs, I'll bargain with you," started the escapee displaying the fruit. "I'll let both you and the dog go, if you show Col and Ben how you can perform with your arkana. You tell your dingo to sit down. I'll place this pear on his head. And from a distance of thirty paces, you throw your arkana at the fruit on his head. If your boomerang cuts it in half, you go free."

"What!" reacted Yurgama, aghast and worried. "Even if I could do it, what guarantee do I have that you will keep your word?"

"You just do it," commanded Boar roar. Yurgama submitted. Col and Ben released him.

The escapee handed him the arkana.

"Don't try to use your fancy stick on us, or I'll put a bullet in the dog," warned the escapee, showing the Trooper a loaded rifle.

Marakorpa obediently sat down at his Master's command and the drama took place. When Yurgama reached his instructed position from the dingo, the three men did their best to distract him. To add to his worries, his pet kept moving his head and the placed pear fell off it. When the fruit was put back, Marakorpa still kept turning his head. All the time and very anxiously, Yurgama held his arkana back in a round arm fashion, aimed and ready to throw.

At last he did throw it and the boomerang sliced off the top part of the pear.

When the implement returned to him, the Aborigine put it back in his belt and looked at Boar roar.

"I've carried out my part of your bargain, Boar roar," he reminded him.

"Do it again. Just to show Col and Ben it wasn't a fluke," suggested the escapee tauntingly. The other two men laughed approvingly.

The Aborigine paused, pretending to consider the suggestion. To his relief, Marakorpa had wandered off out of sight. Apparently something in the bush must have attracted the dingo.

The men grew impatient. Ben moved menacingly close to Yurgama. Then, before they could do anything about it the Aborigine grabbed the pot-bellied fellow.

"You've asked for it, Jacobs," said Boar roar and he fired the rifle at the Trooper. But Yurgama used Ben as a shield. He managed to swing him around and the bullet penetrated his stomach.

As he collapsed with an agonised grunt to the ground, Yurgama went with him. Boar roar loaded his rifle again, while Col stood timidly and hesitantly.

But before the big escapee could pull the rifle trigger again, the Aborigine was able to roll onto his side, whip his arkana from his belt and throw it hard at him. The steel-rimmed implement cut deeply into Boar roar's throat. With a screech of pain, he fell to the ground.

Despairingly, Col jumped on his horse and fled. Yurgama never found out what became of him.

The Trooper wondered whether he could get Doctor Wudder in time to attend to the two seriously injured men. But both Boar roar and Ben died.

Searching around the bush, the Aborigine found Marakorpa. An irritated blue tongue lizard was putting up with the attentions of the curious dingo.

Contrasting Offenders

Drizzling, drenching rain had fallen for three days in Tilabrook. As a result, Jessel Parade was thick with mud.

In Jessel Parade, a commotion was taking place, which was attracting the attention of concerned onlookers.

One of the citizens went into the Police Station and reported the situation to Yurgama.

When he went out, the black Trooper saw the situation as the citizen had described it.

A dray-load of wool, being pulled by four bullocks, was stranded in the mud. The driver was impatiently, mercilessly whipping his team to keep moving. Alongside him, a young lady was appealing to him to stop hitting the animals.

Approaching, Yurgama appealed too. But the man would not listen to anyone.

The Aborigine took his arkana from his belt and threw it, just as the driver was about to strike the beasts again. The outside of the curved implement knocked the whip out of the man's hand.

Infuriated, he picked it up and shouted at Yurgama as the Aborigine's arkana returned to him.

"You interfering Trooper. I have a deadline to meet, to get this wool to Melbourne. What are you trying to do?"

"Why don't you have a look to see what is holding up your

dray, instead of belting those beasts?" said the Aborigine.

"Why don't you mind your own business?" admonished the man.

"Please control yourself, Uncle Brendan," advised the girl next to him.

"If you like, I'll have a look at the dray and see what the trouble is, Miss," offered Yurgama.

"You just stay away, or I'll crack you with this leather," threatened the driver.

The Aborigine took no notice and started to go forward.

The man carried out his threat and attempted to lash the Trooper with his whip. But Yurgama saw his intended movement. The Aborigine threw his arkana again. And again it knocked the whip out of the driver's hand.

In a rage, the man got off the dray and rushed at the Trooper. He tried to punch him in the face. Yurgama grabbed his wrist to ward him off. They ended up wrestling on the muddy ground.

Eventually, the Aborigine subdued his aggressor. Annoyed, he locked him up in one of the Police Station cells.

Later, the girl came in with dry clothes for him. "Could you let Uncle Brendan have a shower and get into these clothes," she requested of Yurgama.

"I don't know whether he deserves such good treatment," reacted the Aborigine, still annoyed.

"You've enjoyed the comfort of washing and changing your clothes. Let my uncle. I know what you are thinking. He isn't a bad man at all. You looked and saw that a rock was stopping the dray wheel from turning. Normally Uncle Brendan would have looked. But he was tired. He panicked. We are running short of time and if he doesn't get the wool to the city on time, he will lose his job."

"Your appeal and charm has won me over, Miss?"

"Moylan, Emily Moylan," answered the girl.

"And what's your uncle's surname?" asked the Aborigine.

"Moylan, too."

Another Station cell was occupied by a middle-aged fellow with a liquor problem—Gavin Shaw.

Shaw was a bachelor who worked irregularly. When he saved enough money, he would spend it all at once. This led to over-indulgence in beer at the Magpie Hotel, which was followed by the bachelor misbehaving and ending up in the Police Station for a night.

Yurgama had tried to reform him. The Reverend Chopadick had tried to reform him.

On this night, the Aborigine made him an offer. "Gavin, you can leave here, if you will read a part of the Bible which the Reverend Chopadick requested of you."

"I'll do it," agreed Shaw.

"I suppose it is only a few pages," he remarked as Yurgama opened up the Holy Scriptures. The Trooper pointed out the section which the Minister wanted the bachelor to read.

"What! That's twenty-five pages. It will take me ages to read," said Shaw.

"Have a go," suggested the Aborigine.

Shaw settled down to study. He was on the other side of the Trooper's desk. Marakorpa was asleep on the floor. And as the clock on the Station wall ticked away, the Aborigine fell asleep in his chair, too.

Bored, Gavin Shaw looked up from the Bible.

He noticed on a string on the wall at the back of him, the key to the Police Station's back door. He decided he would use it.

But as he tiptoed over and went to take the key, Marakorpa

made a yawning noise. It woke Yurgama. He saw what Shaw was doing and tossed the arkana.

The bachelor had just lifted the string on which the key dangled, when the steel-rimmed implément cut it. The key dropped to the floor as the implement returned to land on the desk.

A jolted Shaw looked at Yurgama who was grinning.

"I couldn't resist doing that, Gavin," informed the Trooper.

"Yur, I did do some reading," said the bachelor.

"All right, you can go. I wish you would see the fruitlessness of over-drinking."

"We only live once, mate," were the concluding departing words of the bachelor.

The next morning, Brendan Moylan apologised to Yurgama.

"I'm sincerely sorry for the trouble I caused, Trooper. I'm willing to face charges and the consequences for my offences."

"You're forgiven, Brendan. Your niece spoke up for you too. The bullocks have been well-fed and rested. They should get your wool to Melbourne on time," said the Aborigine.

"I'm deeply grateful to you," reacted the bullock driver. "You can be sure that my misbehaviour was not my normal behaviour."

"I'm sure it wasn't," supported Yurgama. "I have a frequent visitor to these cells, who unfortunately doesn't see the error of his ways," commented the Aborigine, referring to Gavin Shaw.

The Warmth of Wendy

In a fall on a flight of stairs, Mrs Oenone Cushing had broken a leg. Doctor Eric Wudder said that it would be several weeks before she could walk again.

While his wife was incapacitated, Fedor Cushing employed a girl to do the housework and cook meals.

Fedor was an accountant in Tilabrook and his birthday was drawing near at the time. Oenone gave the girl some money and asked her to buy a gift for her husband.

The lass went into the Vaducon Men's Tailors to look for something suitable. In the clothes shop, Yurgama was buying socks.

"Excuse me," he said to the girl. "Are you working for the Cushings?"

"Yes," she answered.

"I'm a friend of theirs. How is Mrs Cushing?"

"She is as good as gold. She just has to wait for nature to take its course and her leg to mend up."

"I haven't seen you around here before. Do you live in the district?"

"No, I'm from Melbourne and Holland originally. I wanted to get away from the big town for awhile. And I gained this job helping out the Cushings. You look like the local Trooper."

"Yes," said Yurgama with a nod.

"What is your race? Are you a native of New Guinea?"

"No, Aboriginal. My name is Yurgama Jacobs."

"I'm Wendy Van Emerick, Mr Jacobs. I suppose I had better keep looking around the shop. I've got to buy something for Mr Cushing. It's his birthday soon."

"Wendy, before I go, would you feel like having dinner with me at the Station? I live there."

The girl paused to consider the unexpected invitation.

"Yes, I'd love to," she answered with an enthusiastic smile. "Every now and again, the Cushings give me a night off from cooking the evening meal. And tonight I am free."

"Do you know where the Police Station is?"

"Yes, I've passed it. It's only a quick walk from the Cushing's home in Jessel Parade."

"Would seven o'clock suit you to come?"

"Yes, that would be fine."

"Terrific," reacted the Aborigine. "I'm not much of a cook. But I hope I can dish up something edible."

"I'll give you a few cooking hints," offered Wendy lightly.

"Good," said Yurgama with a departing smile.

"Bye for now, and thanks," she farewelled.

Wendy Van Emerick was a skinny girl with a pure, light tan skin, brown hair, brown eyes and a self-assured, friendly face.

To Yurgama's delight, she fulfilled his invitation that evening. During her stay, Marakorpa found out that she liked dogs, and he pressed her for much affectionate attention which she readily gave.

Through the next fortnight, the Aborigine three times repeated an invitation to the girl to have dinner at the Station with him and each time she accepted.

With the loan of a pony, they went riding in the bush. Though Wendy had never ridden before, she proved to be a surprisingly confident, competent horsewoman.

That night, there was a thunderstorm. The weather got bitterly cold. Yurgama built up the fire in his living room, while Wendy delayed her return to the Cushings till the rain cleared.

Marakorpa stretched out on a rug near the hearth of the fire. Yurgama moved a settee closer to it. He and Wendy sat down and warmed their hands.

Up till now, the couple had never touched each other. They settled back to watch the yellow flames leaping up through the chimney.

Pleasantly tired, Wendy moved closer to the Trooper. She slipped her hand behind his back, around his waist and rested her head on his shoulder.

Yurgama felt a thrill at her touch. He put his arm around her slender shoulder and drew her enjoyably closer.

He instinctively moved to hold her small hand and press his cheek against her forehead.

On a sunnier day they went riding again. Tethering the horses to a tree out of Tilabrook, they sat down on a rock. The sky above was rich blue and cloudless.

"Wendy, when did you leave Holland?" asked the Trooper.

"When I was thirteen," answered the girl.

"You have no accent in speaking English."

"I can speak and write ten languages."

"You're deceiving me," said Yurgama.

"Yes, I can," reassured the girl. I know Dutch, English, Spanish, French, German, Norwegian, Italian, Polish, Hungarian and Rumanian."

"What an unusual gift. It's hard to believe. You're not very old. How did you come to master them?”

“They fascinated me. At a library in Amsterdam, there happened to be books on these languages. I spent all my spare time reading them and I was able to learn what I read.”

For seven weeks, the Dutch girl and the Aborigine continued their association.

In the eighth week, she made an unplanned visit to the Police Station.

“Yurgama.”

“Hello Wendy.”

“Mrs Cushing’s leg is better. She is walking freely now. My job with them is finished.”

“Are you returning to Melbourne?” asked the Trooper dismayed.

“I don’t want to go. I want to stay here with you.”

“You’re a lovely girl. I’ve got deeply fond of you. I’ll miss you.”

“Yurgama, say the word and I’ll be your wife.”

“There is nothing I’d like better, Wendy. But I mustn’t. For you to become my wife in a small country town like this, would be a waste of your talent.”

“What do you mean?”

“I’m talking about your ability to speak and write so many languages. You could go to England and use that ability in the services of someone like Her Majesty The Queen. She must have to relate to other European monarchs and dignitaries.”

The couple put their arms around each other and kissed long and tenderly.

Two days later at the Cobb & Co Depot, Fedor and Oenone Cushing and Yurgama farewelled Wendy as she was about to leave for Melbourne.

The Dutch girl and the Aborigine hugged for as long as possible. They had to finally release each other when the coach driver called all passengers to get aboard.

Wendy went to England and got a position in the Prime Minister's Foreign Department, which used her linguistic talent to the full. She remained in this position for the rest of her life and married an Englishman.

Night Prowler

The funeral of Mrs Alice Slater was held at Saint Bartholomew's Anglican Church in Tilabrook.

Mrs Slater, a widow, had lived with her only son Kerry. She was buried at the Tilabrook cemetery. Yurgama, who knew the family well, acted as one of the pall bearers. Twenty-two-year-old Kerry wept all through his mother's service.

He was a carpenter by trade and had supported his mother whom he was dearly devoted to. Though Kerry was a hand-some, broad-shouldered boy, he cultivated no friendships with people of his own age and always sought his mother's protective love. With concern, she gave him the maternal care he desired of her. Now she was gone.

The black Trooper went to see Kerry and asked him if there was anything he could do for him.

Two nights later, on a Thursday, Yurgama, in the early hour of the morning, retired to bed. He pondered on the future of the boy who had taken his mother's death so badly. Just as he was about to fall off to sleep, the Aborigine thought he heard a noise. He looked at the window and there appeared to be what looked like a man peering in.

Startled, the Aborigine rushed out. But he did not see any-one around. With puzzlement, he was just about to go back in, when there was a further noise. From around a corner, there was an approaching moonlit shadow. However, the Trooper was able to relax. It turned out to be Marakorpa. The Aborigine had forgotten to let him in for the night.

But when Yurgama returned to bed, his sleep was unpleasant. He had a series of nightmares of figures haunting him at the window. In one dream, a figure appeared to come into the room and bear down on him. He struggled to awaken, but at first could not move his body. When he did, he discovered his body was hot and sweating. There was perspiration on his brow.

In the morning, he concluded from his experience in the night that no prowler had invaded his privacy. It was a part of his bad dreams.

But in each week that followed, reports came to the Police Station from Tilabrook citizens. The reports were the same. Late at night, somebody had disturbed the people by appearing at a window of their home. Hence, Yurgama had not dreamt about his intruder.

After about four weeks, the citizens felt alarmed. The disturbances had continued. The culprit had not been caught.

A meeting was called in the Town Hall for male citizens. Yurgama had earlier stayed up two nights patrolling the streets. Now five of the men present at the meeting, who were bachelors, volunteered to do a night guard.

But they seemed to patrol on the wrong nights and the prowler remained on the loose.

There was growing concern for the safety of the women and children. What kind of man was this night stalker? Sooner or later, would he do something violent?

One day, Kerry Slater walked into the Police Station. The

black Trooper did not know whether he was imagining it or not, but the expression in the boy's eyes appeared eerily odd.

"Yurgama," he said.

"Hello Kerry," acknowledged the Aborigine.

"I have heard about this prowler."

"A bit of a nuisance, isn't he? Are you starting to feel better since Mama died?"

"Yes."

There was a pause. Marakorpa, who had been asleep, looked up and saw the boy. The dingo let out a long growl.

"Korpa! Keep quiet!" admonished the Trooper. "What's the matter with you? You know Kerry."

"Yurgama, there is something I'd like to say," said the boy.

"I'm surprised at Korpa. It's not like him to growl at anyone. What did you say Kerry?"

Again there was a pause as the Aborigine waited on the pondering young man to speak.

"Oh, it doesn't matter, Yur. You're busy. I think I'll go," he said at last.

Perplexed, Yurgama watched him quietly leave.

The Trooper took another look at Marakorpa and shrugged his shoulders, mystified.

The Aborigine wrote down the details of all the reports and complaints that came in about the prowler's continuing disturbances. The Trooper studied the details. After six weeks, he discovered there was a sequence. The Tilabrook peace disturber came out once a week. Every report showed that he came out on a Thursday, in the earliest hour of the morning. In each case, the disturbed residents had retired for the night and were unable to recognise the man's face. But he was broad-shouldered and appeared to have undone hair.

"It couldn't be," thought Yurgama to himself. The description fitted Kerry Slater. There was only one way to find out if Kerry was the culprit.

In the earliest hour of the following Thursday morning, the Aborigine waited in Jessel Parade.

At precisely 12:30, somebody came into the dark, quiet street. Yurgama hid and watched him. To the lawman's disappointment it appeared obvious that it was Kerry Slater. He followed the boy, who went into a side street. He saw him climb the picket fence of a home. The young man sealed his guilt when he approached a window of the house. The Aborigine called to him. He turned around shocked and thought of dashing off.

"Don't run away, Kerry," requested the Trooper.

"Yurgama, I was going to confess to you that day."

"Keep your voice down, mate."

"I just want to see Mama again."

"Come to the Station and we will talk about it."

At the Station:

"On the night Mama died, I had this dream, Yurgama," explained the young man. "Mama appeared to me in the dream. She said I could see her. She instructed me to seek her in people's homes on a Thursday night. She said she would talk to me then."

"And have you seen her?" asked the Trooper.

"No, but I will."

"Kerry, you just had a crazy dream. You don't want to take any notice of it."

"But I must. I must see Mama again. She was so good and so beautiful. I need her, Yur, I won't cause any harm to people."

Kerry had to be kept in an asylum in Melbourne. Twice he escaped and tried to get to Tilabrook to fulfil his dream.

After some time, Denise Hegerty, a Warrnambool girl, met the young man and fell in love with him. With much failure, she tried to make him see that his thinking was off balance. It seemed there was no hope for the young carpenter.

But after four years, he came to realise that his thinking was wrong,

He and Denise married and lived in Warrnambool. Their married life lasted sixty-three years, before Kerry died. In that time, the couple had fifteen children.

Our Rainbow

A new assistant teacher had arrived in Tilabrook for the Primary School. She was Mabel Enton, a girl from Geelong. Mabel was staying with Miss Faddin who lived with her mother.

When Yurgama first saw Mabel Enton, he got a surprise at her height. The Aborigine was six feet tall and Miss Enton would have been at least as tall.

The girl had been told about the local Trooper and when they met, she said, "You must be Yurgama Jacobs."

"Yes, and you must be Miss Mabel Enton," he replied with a smile.

"I've heard you have some sort of special instrument. Is that it?" she remarked, looking at Yurgama's arkana,

He invited her to go into the Magpie Hotel with him and he said he would give her a demonstration with his boomerang.

In the hotel, he handed a shilling piece to the bartender who greeted him jovially. He asked the bartender to give him twelve pennies change.

Mabel Enton watched the Trooper as he placed the copper coins in a row, at twelve inch spaces, along a twenty foot bench.

Then, at one end of the bench, the Aborigine tossed his arkana just above the counter. As his boomerang returned to him, the curved implement slid along the bench knocking each of the pennies onto the floor.

"Bravo! You ought to join a circus," reacted Mabel cheekily, but light-heartedly. She raised her hands and clapped briefly.

"I was in a circus before I joined the Police Force," informed the Aborigine.

After that initial meeting, he sought the companionship of the girl from Geelong.

When she first saw Marakorpa, she was tentative about patting him.

"Will be bite?" she asked the Aborigine, who confirmed to her that his pet was very placid.

One Sunday, the teacher and the Trooper had a barbecue in the country. Yurgama chose a spot for their outing on high ground, where there was a good view of surrounding scenery.

After they had enjoyed steak and tomatoes and tea and cake, the Aborigine insisted on cleaning up.

He looked up to notice the girl standing motionless, a short distance from him. Most of her back was facing him, as she seemed to be taking in the view. For the first time, he looked at her intently. Her dark brown hair was short-cropped. Her shoulders and hips were well-proportioned. She stood tall and beautiful. From what he could see of her pretty face, the Aborigine detected loneliness in her.

An overpowering urge swept through him. He got up and went to her. He wanted to hold her, kiss her passionately and love her.

Drawing closer, he took hold of her arms and she started momentarily. He turned her around, held her tightly. She looked at him submissively. He moved his lips to hers.

"No!" she cried and sharply released herself from his hold. She moved away a few paces.

"I'm sorry, Mabel," said the Trooper.

"You did no wrong, Yurgama," she said, making him feel at ease. "I want to be close friends with you. But I don't want you to ever try to kiss me the way you intended."

"Why?" asked the Aborigine softly.

"I'm going into an Adelaide convent next year. I'm going to become a nun."

"I didn't know," apologised the Trooper. "That's all right," accepted the girl.

"Are you sure that is what you want to do with your life, Mabel?"

"I'm positive. I was brought up in a very ardently Catholic family. Two uncles are priests. I firmly believe in my faith. I believe God has called me to a religious vocation."

On another Sunday, on another outing, the tall Geelong lass and Yurgama went into the country again.

It was an ill-chosen day, for rain had fallen intermittently. However, the couple managed to find shelter under huge rocks. There they talked.

"Yurgama," began the girl. "Your arkana looks as though it could injure, maim or even kill?"

"Yes," answered the Aborigine solemnly.

"Have you ever killed anyone with it?"

"In self defence or the defence of others," said the Trooper.

The girl seemed to accept his answer.

"Life at present is untamed, Mabel. It can be violent, and unfortunately, there sometimes isn't a gentle way to cope with that violence."

At this moment, a sun-shower was coming to a stop. One part of the sky was a deep grey colour.

"Look over there," pointed out Yurgama.

"There's a rainbow."

"Our rainbow," remarked Mabel, warmly looking at the Trooper.

"Our rainbow till next year when I lose you. But in the meantime, you'll love me," said the Aborigine.

"Yes!" declared the tall girl definitely. And she put her white hand over his black hand.

Buxom Beauty

On a Saturday in May, a gala occasion was to take place in Tilabrook. There was to be a race meeting with three events, including the inaugural Tilabrook Cup. Sideline entertainment included a kite-flying contest for youngsters.

Harry and Olive Pexter and their two sons, Sam and Des, were very much involved in the occasion.

Harry was the owner and trainer of the top-weight horse in the Tilabrook Cup race. She was a black thoroughbred mare with the name Buxom Beauty. In the race, she was to carry nine stone six pounds, which was pounds more than the next horse.

Sam and Des Pexter, boys in their early teens, had spent much time and effort in making their entry for the kite-flying contest.

Yurgama thought of taking Marakorpa to the race meeting on a leash, but he finally decided to leave his pet at home, thinking that the dingo would restrict his movements.

In the morning, before the meeting in the afternoon, cause for worry occurred for the Pexters. Frank Attaway, the young jockey who was to ride Buxom Beauty, reported that the horse had been limping. He thought it may have been due to an injury to her fetlock.

"We must not risk causing serious damage to Buxom. It

looks as though we will have to withdraw her from the race," declared Harry Pexter with sad resignation.

A suitable breeze was blowing when the kite-flying contest took place in the middle of the racecourse, to open the afternoon's program. There were many entries of differing shapes, sizes, patterns and colours. Sam and Des had by far the biggest kite.

A large crowd of people from the town and surrounding districts were present. Harry and Olive were with Yurgama while they watched their sons display their entry which was made from wood and newspaper.

Des, the younger of the two boys, was holding the string on which their large kite flew. The breeze developed into a strong wind.

Unexpectedly, Des was lifted off the ground.

Sam made a lunge to grab onto the kite string to add his weight and pull it down. But he missed.

To the surprise of those people watching, Des was elevated into the air. When he was about five feet off the ground, his mother anxiously asked Yurgama to throw his arkana.

The Aborigine and the Pexters were a fair distance away. But quickly, the black Trooper took his boomerang from his belt and threw it hard and high. In its flight, it snapped the kite string in half, before returning to land at the Aborigine's feet.

Young Des Pexter fell to the ground. He was unhurt. But both he and Sam felt disappointed about losing their large entry which flew out of sight through the sky.

However, news came forward to brighten the Pexters. Half an hour before the main race, in the middle of the afternoon, Frank Attaway reported that Buxom Beauty was not limping. She was moving completely freely.

"If it's not too late, we will start her, Frank," said Harry.

It was not too late. Buxom Beauty took her place with nine other horses at the commencement of the Tilabrook Cup.

The starter set them on their way for the mile and a half distance. The jockeys got their mounts away evenly and without difficulty.

For the first part of the race, the horses were bunched together. Then Great Conqueror, a fawn coloured gelding and the favourite for the event, drew away to take the lead.

With only half a mile left, Great Conqueror increased his lead by two lengths.

Buxom Beauty had the energy to increase her speed, but she was trapped on the rails behind three other horses. Frank Attaway was about to give up hope of winning.

However, one of the horses ahead of the Pexter mare, tired badly and left an opening.

Frank did not fail to use it. Buxom Beauty overtook four horses within seconds.

With a quarter of a mile to go, she was ahead of the main group and one and a half lengths behind Great Conqueror.

As they got closer to the winning post, the black mare drew level with the fawn gelding. The crowd cheered with the excitement.

Three times, Great Conqueror or Buxom Beauty got their head in front of the other.

But Buxom Beauty's winning heart was big. In the last moments, she drew away to win the race by half a neck from Great Conqueror on the rail.

"Buxom's a beauty indeed. I didn't have to use the whip on her once," declared Frank Attaway to the thrilled Pexters.

The donor of the Tilabrook Cup was Sir Martin Vaducon. He

presented a silver trophy and twenty-five guineas prize money to Harry Pexter.

Sam and Des were made to feel better about the loss of their kite. Their entry was judged to be the best and they received a small, valuable trophy.

Buxom Beauty went on to win many races for the Pexters and gave them pride and pleasure. The black mare's races included five starts in events at Flemington in Melbourne, and she won three of them.

The Kimberleys to Kimberley

A research and exploration party made a voyage around Australia for a planned period of eighteen months.

Yurgama accompanied the party as a security guard. While away, the black Trooper left Marakorpa in the care of friends in Tilabrook.

On the voyage, the party saw the rugged countryside of the Kimberleys. The scientific team went ashore and one of their members discovered man-like foot marks in the earth. It was considered that they appeared unlikely to belong to natives. The suggestion was made that Yurgama follow the prints.

The Trooper said that he was as qualified as a near-sighted platypus to be an Aboriginal tracker. However, he undertook the task. He was as curious as the rest of the party about who the foot marks belonged to.

He followed them, and they came to appear along the side of a stream. The sun was humidly hot. The Trooper took a rest and quenched his thirst at the stream.

Unknowingly, his track following led him to come between a wedge-tailed eagle and her nest of young ones.

The giant bird prepared to attack from its position in a far distant tree. Yurgama saw the looming danger. He whipped his arkana from his belt and threw it. It struck a wing of the flying eagle.

The antagonised, wounded brown wedgetail was temporarily stopped.

As Yurgama picked up his returned implement, he thought fearfully of the pain and bloodshed, the eagle's talons could cause.

For a moment, the Trooper thought he could relax. But the giant bird flew in. It was almost upon the man when he managed to lash decisively with his steel-rimmed boomerang.

But the powerful wedge-tail, though it was wounded a second time, still had much strength and fighting determination.

It flew at Yurgama again and again. He lashed at it repeatedly with his arkana till his arm ached and perspiration trickled from his brow.

Some of the blows made contact. But in one attack from the bird, it's talons came within less than an inch of ripping the Aborigine's forearm. He felt he could no longer stand up to the onslaught. Then, a tired, but well-directed lash with the arkana cut into the relentless wedgetail's neck and finally killed it.

Exhausted, the Trooper sat down and panted.

He felt relieved and also sad at having had to destroy such a magnificent bird.

It was not long after he resumed the tracking, when a combination of his torrid experience and the severe heat caused Yurgama to collapse.

The Aborigine's body lay still in the sun till a shadow appeared over it. The shadow was of a white man—long-bearded, bedraggled, but sturdy. His instant thought was how he could help the unconscious Trooper.

Unperturbed at the required heavy effort, the long-bearded

fellow picked up the Aborigine and leaned him over his shoulder. Taking periodic rests, he carried the Trooper over two miles to a hut in a tree-filled gorge near the ocean.

When he returned to consciousness, Yurgama was naturally surprised at seeing the man and the surroundings. The Trooper noticed that the marks made in the ground by the fellow's makeshift footwear, were the same as the marks the Aborigine had been tracking.

With sign language and drawings in the dirt, the two men were able to communicate roughly. Not being sure, Yurgama thought the fellow was probably the survivor of a shipwreck.

His assumption was to prove correct. The other members of the research party, concerned at the Trooper's delayed absence, looked for him. They were able to follow the tracks he left behind and come upon the long-bearded man's hut, after following his burdened footsteps.

One of the party, a Dutchman, soon found out that the stranger spoke his language.

The bedraggled man related his story.

His name was Hank Kalff. He was a Dutch East Indies official. He was aboard a ship sailing for Africa where he hoped to rejoin his sweetheart, Beatrix Van Osterwick in Cape Town.

The ship was sailing near the Kimberleys from Timor. A tidal wave caused by a cylcone sank the vessel.

With two other men, Hank managed to get to shore. But one of the fellows was so weak from the experience that he died and the other man committed suicide.

Hence, Hank was left on his own.

Driven by the hope to see his beloved Beatrix again, he determined to survive in the desolate country.

The three survivors had managed to get some possessions

to shore as well as themselves. Hank made use of these possessions. He built his hut and lived off natural vegetation and wildlife. From the seasonal climatic changes, he guessed that he could have been in the Kimberleys a year.

Gratefully, he joined the research party for the rest of their voyage.

After some time of working and saving in Melbourne, Hank finally got to Cape Town. There, he found Beatrix operating a thriving hotel business. However, with true love and many moments when she thought Hank would never come; that she would never see him again, she had nevertheless waited for him.

They married and spent a holiday in Kimberley with friends of Beatrix.

During this stay, Hank discovered a hard, glass-like stone. He was sure it was a diamond. He took it to an expert who confirmed that it was genuine.

The man pressed his bride to sell her hotel. He wanted them to concentrate their finances on first buying the land where he discovered the stone and then mining that land.

Beatrix was sceptical. Her husband's ideas seemed absurd, too vulnerable to failure, to losing all the assets they had. But she relented.

They got the land for a cheap price. Hank spent much money paying men with knowledge of mining, employing many labourers and buying equipment and materials.

Time marched on. The mining went deeper. But no diamonds were found. The Kalff's money was running out fast. Already many labourers' wages were overdue.

The enterprise had failed. Beatrix was sorrowful. Hank felt extreme depression and despair at having let his wife down.

The couple argued heatedly. Beatrix decided to leave her husband. He could face the financial mess alone. Cousins in Cape Town were ready to let her live with them.

But just as she packed her belongings and was on the point of leaving, a labourer walked into the Kalff house. He strongly advised Hank to give up the gamble immediately, when a small glass-like stone fell from the fellow's pocket onto the floor.

The labourer said he found it while mining. He took possession of it out of fascination, but did not think it was valuable. He said the workers had come upon a couple of other similar type stones. Hence, he was surprised when Hank jumped for joy.

Beatrix was unsure. But her husband enthusiastically persuaded her to give him another chance.

It was soon proved that the miners had found the sought-after gemstone. The enterprise was saved. The Kalff's financial troubles were mended, their marriage was mended and they came to reap much wealth.

Back in Australia, before the research party left the Kimberleys with Hank, Yurgama told about his battle with the eagle. The Aborigine gave his suggestion as to why the wedgetail attacked him; that the bird thought her young ones were in danger from him. He had seen the nest.

With the intention of not abandoning the motherless young eagles to die, the party went back to rescue them. They were taken aboard the research team's ship. One member, Ted O'Shea took on the task of nurturing the two big baby birds.

He was a squatter with a sheep grazing property near Deniliquin in New South Wales. He called the young eagles "Browny" and "Arrogance".

As the pet wedgetails grew to full growth, they came to be able to get their own food.

Ted had freed the large, handsome eagles. However, intermittently they returned to his homestead and received food scraps from the dinner table.

Elstan

On a sunny, but fresh spring day, Yurgama rode on his chestnut hack at a steady pace through countryside near Tilabrook. He looked around to notice that Marakorpa had lagged behind out of sight. He whistled, but there was no response from the dingo.

Retracing his tracks, the Trooper found his pet sniffing at something on the ground. It was a tiny baby bird without any feathers. Yurgama surmised that it must have fallen from a nest in a tree nearby. He picked the helpless little bird up with the intention of taking it home and nurturing it.

Where his new found pet could be safe, the Aborigine kept it in a cage in his living room. He fed the tiny orphan with finely cut up bread, milk and honey. He handled the bird (a male finch) a lot, talked to it and gave it the name Elstan,

As Elstan began to get feathers, he became a noisily happy bird and expressed a pretty musical chirp. When he gained all his feathers, which were yellow on the breast and grey on his back, he flew about his cage.

After making sure the window and doors were closed, Yurgama one day let the little finch loose in the living room.

After flying about in an uncertain manner, Elstan picked his first landing spot to be Marakorpa's nose. The dingo made no movement or reaction. He was stunned with surprise.

Yurgama called Elstan, and after flying a few further times in a circle about the room, the little bird came to stand on the Aborigine's shoulder.

The Trooper let his feathered friend out of the cage frequently from then on. He was to find that the bird was quite delightfully intelligent as well as tame.

Once, when Elstan was standing on the living room mantelpiece, Yurgama threw a match up in the air near the bird. It caught the match in its beak, then proceeded to go along the mantelpiece tossing the firelighter up in the air and catching the stick in its mouth.

Once, Yurgama had prepared himself a nice hot mug of tea. He settled down in an armchair in the living room and proceeded to stir the sugar he had put in the tea.

With anticipated satisfaction, he moved the mug to his lips, to take a sip. A small bomb dropped from above and made a minor splash in the beverage. It was one of Elstan's untimely droppings.

"That's the end of that nice drink," declared Yurgama to himself, as he proceeded to go out and dispose of the beverage.

He increased the variety of Elstan's diet. As the bird became fully grown, the Aborigine decided to take the risk and let it fly outside.

Unaccustomed to this strange new world, the little finch was reluctant to leave Yurgama's person.

The trooper felt he might be jeopardising his new pet's safety. But, when Elstan at last was tempted by curiosity as well as courage to leave Yurgama, he did not fly too far for too long.

In his new, bigger world, the bird got Marakorpa interested in playing a game in which the dingo was always the loser. Elstan would fly up in the air with a small twig in his beak and drop the twig above Marakorpa. The animal would try to catch the wood in his mouth. But just as it fell within a few inches of his eager mouth, the little bird would swoop down and catch the twig in its beak again.

After a while, Marakorpa would give the game away through defeated tiredness. But like a fool, the dingo always came back on future occasions to be a loser at Elstan's game.

One day, little John Hump junior came to see the local peacekeeper:—

"Yurgama, I've heard you have a pet bird."

"Yes John."

"Would you be interested in selling him?"

"Would you give him a good home and look after him?"

"Yes, for sure. You just tell us how to care for him and name your selling price."

"You can have him for nothing, John."

"Fair dinkum?"

"Fair dinkum."

Elstan was put in his cage and his new young guardian took it preciously.

But barely a week had passed, when Sabrina went into the Police Station upset.

"Yurgama! Elstan is missing!"

"Since when Sabrina?"

"John took a gamble and let him outside for the first time this morning."

"It was dull and overcast this morning. It looked as though we may have fog before the day is through."

"It is terrible foggy outside now. It's so thick, you can hardly see a foot in front of you."

The Aborigine had remained in the Station doing desk work,

so he felt certain that the finch had not flown back to its old home.

"We'll find Elstan, Sabrina," he said cheerfully and optimistically to the little girl. He went to the Hump's home with her.

By the late afternoon, the fog had well and truly cleared. But the little finch was still nowhere to be found. Sabrina cried, but Yurgama pressed her not to give up hope that Elstan would be all right.

The Aborigine left the little girl and her disappointed brother John with their parents.

But not long after, in his living room, the first scene to catch the Trooper's eyes was Elstan.

Marakorpa was dozing on his side and the little finch was perched asleep on the dingo's neck.

Yurgama tiptoed out and rushed to the home. He wanted the children to see the scene in the living room and he carried a red-eyed Sabrina back enthusiastically.

Strangled

The well-attired, well-built man stood near the footpath outside the Tilabrook Police Station. He was peeling a banana and gazing nonchalantly down the street. A window of the Station was wide open and Yurgama, glancing at the man, came with pleasure to recognise him to be a childhood friend, Dick Olsen.

The Aborigine's instant thought was to go out and greet him immediately. But he thought that before he did, he would play a prank on his mate.

He threw his arkana through the window and it sliced off the top half of Olsen's banana.

The well-clad man's head jolted back with surprise, as the arkana sailed back through the window and the black Trooper kept out of sight.

With a broad grin, the Aborigine went out to greet his old friend.

"Yurgama! I thought I saw a flash of a steel-rimmed boomerang. But then I was puzzled. I didn't think you were the peace officer in Tilabrook," said Olsen, warmly patting the Trooper's shoulder as the two shook hands.

"It's been years since I laid eyes on you, Dick. But I recognised you immediately."

"The kid who taught you how to wrestle and box. How could you forget," remarked Olsen.

"And always beat me," added the Aborigine with a smile.

"How are your parents these days, Yur?"

"Gone to heaven, Dick. Come into the Station. I'm not busy. We'll have a cup of tea. I'll make up for that half banana that you can't eat."

"Okay, thanks," accepted Olsen walking ahead of his friend.

"How long have you been in Tilabrook?" asked the Trooper when they were inside the sandstone building.

"Just arrived today on the coach. I've come to see a friend, Vivien Cameron."

"Ah, the lass who runs the small lady's dress shop in Jessel Parade. I suppose you're a guest at her coming wedding."

"Wedding!" Dick Olsen was shocked.

"Yes," confirmed Yurgama. "She is marrying Milton Bunnet, a wheat farmer in the district. If ever a couple make a happy marriage, I reckon they will."

"Excuse me, Yur. I'd better forget that cup of tea for the time being."

"What! Where are you going?"

"I've just thought of some business I have to attend to. I'll see you later," farewelled Olsen.

Before the Trooper could press him to stay, his attention was diverted to a commotion in the Police Station kitchen. Going straight there, he found that Marakorpa had apparently chased after a mouse and had the rodent cornered on top of a large flour tin, above a cupboard.

In this situation, the rodent had nowhere to go, but the dingo could not catch him either.

Yurgama took careful aim with his arkana and tossed it. The steel-rimmed implement struck and killed the mouse. The Aborigine quickly picked up his returned boomerang and went forward keeping back Marakorpa, so that he could dispose of the dead rodent which had fallen to the floor.

Half an hour later, news spread around the town: a murder had been committed. Miss Vivien Cameron had been killed in a back room of her shop—according to Doctor Eric Wudder she was strangled.

People had gathered. Dick Olsen who discovered the dead girl called for the crowd's attention.

"You citizens of Tilabrook. I'm only a stranger in the town. But I think you ought to do something about this horrible crime. I was walking past this helpless girl's shop when she was alive. I heard a man speaking angrily to her. She pleaded to him: 'Milton! Let me go! You're hurting me!' Now Tilabrook citizens, only some or all of you would know who this Milton is. When I went to this girl's aid, he rushed out and I discovered her dead—a beautiful, innocent, helpless girl murdered. Are you people going to do something about this despicable crime?"

"The stranger is right," declared Druce Flattery, coming forward out of the crowd. "He doesn't know who the culprit is who committed this murder. But you and I know him."

"Milton Bunnet!" answered a stern elderly lady.

"Right," continued Druce. "You all know what a nice lass Miss Cameron was. Are we going to let her killer go free?"

"No! Let's do justice!" were some of the reactions of the crowd.

Doctor Wudder was still present. "Don't you people think this is a matter for the law?" he said.

"The law's too slow. A bad crime has been committed and Trooper Jacobs isn't here," replied a member of the crowd.

"Well, I'll inform him," said the practitioner.

"Don't bother, Doc," said someone else.

Stirred up, the men needed no second call from Druce

Flattery to get their horses and ride to the Bunnet farm. They included Nigel Exert, Fedor Cushing and Harry Pexter, among other locals.

Eric Wudder's immediate thought was to go to the Police Station. Dick Olsen saw the Doctor's movement and detained him firmly.

"Let me go, young man. I have to inform the Trooper. An innocent man could be lynched," he appealed.

But Dick Olsen continued to detain the Tilabrook medical practitioner, repeatedly telling him what he had already told the crowd earlier.

When Olsen finally let him go his way, Eric Wudder was half convinced of the argument of the stranger. Hence, Yurgama was delayed even further from receiving the news that Milton Bunnet was in danger.

"Why didn't you tell me this earlier, Doc?" complained the Aborigine rushing, after Eric Wudder had had a change of heart and at last went to the Station. "Milton could be dead by now."

The black Trooper galloped at a furious pace on his stallion to the Bunnet wheat farm. A trail of dust was left in the wake of the horse's hooves.

The Trooper could not have arrived at the Bunnet farm any quicker than he did. The mob had put Milton Bunnet astride his horse with his hands tied behind his back. He was underneath the thick limb of a tree with a rope around his neck tied from the limb. The rope was taut.

Druce Flattery was about to slap the horse away. Yurgama dismounted from his sweating chestnut. He whipped his arkana from his belt and threw it hard. Over the mob's heads the implement flew, cut through the rope and returned to the Aborigine's feet.

"Yurgama, what are you doing?" yelled Nigel Exert.

"Lynching is against the law, Nigel," said the Trooper.

"We are carrying out justice Yurgama. Bunnet brutally strangled his fiancée," yelled another man.

"That's for a judge and jury to decide when all the facts have become known." The men quietened down. Yurgama continued. "I know most of you men and you have disappointed me with this barbaric action. I know you are good people. But you have been excited, emotionally stirred up into possibly murdering an innocent man yourselves. I'm taking Milton in. If he is guilty, he is still entitled to a fair trial."

When he was escorted to Tilabrook by the Trooper, the wheat farmer made some claims. He said that he had been home on his farm all that day. He alleged that Dick Olsen had been interested in Vivien Cameron, even though she had tried to discourage him. Olsen, the farmer claimed, had written love letters to Miss Cameron.

In Tilabrook, in Miss Cameron's shop, the Aborigine investigated Milton Bunnet's claims.

They proved true. The Trooper found love letters to the girl from Dick Olsen in Melbourne. One had been received by Miss Cameron only a week before. In this letter, Olsen complained why she had not replied to his correspondence and he told her he was coming to see her.

Yurgama learnt that his childhood friend had stirred the local men up into almost lynching Milton Bunnet. Olsen, detaining Doctor Wudder from seeing the Trooper, the information that Miss Cameron's lover had taken the coach to Hartog, and all the other evidence led Yurgama to the one conclusion.

He released Milton Bunnet and saddled his stallion for a journey to Hartog. The passengers, including Olsen, on the afternoon stage coach to that town would have to stay over night there, before they continued on to Melbourne. This would give the Trooper ample time to catch up to his childhood friend.

Once at Hartog, Yurgama made inquiries as to where he could find Dick Olsen. He had gone for a walk was the information given.

Well into the night, the Aborigine eventually found him. The man was sitting in a brooding fashion under a gum on the outskirts of the town. No one else was about. The Aborigine rode up.

"Dick," he announced.

"Yurgama!" reacted Olsen with surprise.

"You will have to come back to Tilabrook with me, mate. I'm placing you under arrest for Miss Cameron's death," informed the Trooper.

"That's a little silly, Yur. You must have been told who killed her."

"I'd say that after I told you Miss Cameron was marrying another man, you went to her shop in a rage and killed her. Then you aroused the people to kill her fiancé

"A lot of rubbish! You have no evidence."

"Your letters to Miss Cameron for a start."

Dick Olsen reacted anxiously. "Now Yur, you wouldn't arrest an old mate."

"I'm asking you to come with me quietly, Dick."

"What if I don't want to come, mate? There isn't anyone around and if you're to take me, you will have to beat the friend who always, as you put it, beat you in boxing and wrestling when we were kids."

"You're only acknowledging your guilt, Dick," said Yurgama.

Unexpectedly, Olsen rushed at the Aborigine whose chestnut reared up with fright. The Trooper was pulled to the ground by his old friend.

Olsen attempted to deliver quick punches to the lawman's face as he tried to get to his feet. But Yurgama kept dodging. After being able to get in a damaging blow to his adversary's nose, the Aborigine was able to scramble to his feet. Olsen retaliated by rushing at the Trooper's stomach and wrenching his arkana from his belt. The action caused the Aborigine to fall to the ground on his backside near the tree.

His childhood friend stood over him, brandishing the curved implement.

"You've killed people with this boomerang, Yur. Now I'm going to kill you with it."

Olsen swung with the arkana. Yurgama dodged, and the implement wedged into the tree behind.

Desperately, Dick Olsen tried to get the weapon free from the gum. This was Yurgama's chance to subdue his adversary. He drove a left punch to the pit of Olsen's stomach and a right uppercut to his jaw. Quickly, the Tilabrook Trooper put handcuffs on the panting, pained man before he could recover to fight again.

Hard Questions

"Celeste and I are going to celebrate twenty years of marriage with a second honeymoon, Yur. We are going to Melbourne for a week to see some shows, do some dancing and go to the races."

The speaker was Bert Reid, a well-to-do cattle grazier in the Tilabrook district. The black Trooper reacted to his news by remarking that Bert and his wife's planned holiday was well deserved. The Aborigine had just passed by the grazier outside "The Magpie."

"Bert, do you and Mrs Reid feel comfortable about leaving Glen behind to manage the property and look after Clarry?"

Here the Trooper was referring to the Reids' two sons.

"Well, it's a worry, Yur. But only a slight one I think. Glen's eighteen and he's a reliable lad. But if you would trot out to our place once or twice to see if the boys are all right, mate, the wife and I would be grateful."

"No worries," agreed Yurgama.

"Another favour I'd like to ask of you, Yur," said the grazier. "Celeste and I leave for the big city tomorrow. Could I have a loan of your stick? I want to use it in the morning."

"Yes," answered the puzzled Aborigine taking his arkana from his belt and handing it to the man. He wondered what he wanted it for, but did not like to ask.

The next morning at the Station, there was a yell at the door.

"Yur!" It was Bert Reid.

He had to wait a while for the Tilabrook Trooper to come. The lawman was still in bed.

"Oh, it's you, Bert. Sorry. I slept in. I was having a wonderful dream," he declared, at last coming to the door.

"What was it about?" asked the grazier.

"I was riding through the universe on a magic carpet with Cleopatra, the ancient queen of the Nile."

"Sorry I disturbed it. Here's your stick back."

"What did you use it for?" inquired the Trooper.

"You notice I haven't got a beard this morning, Yur?"

"Yes, you're very well clean-shaven."

"It was your stick that did it."

"What!"

"Yes. I misplaced my cutthroat. That's why I got a loan of the boomerang. I thought the steel in it would be sharp enough to take off whiskers and it was."

A few days later, Yurgama went to the Reid cattle property. Soaking up the sun beside the family's red brick home was a big tabby tomcat. As soon as it saw Marakorpa, who had come too, the cat raised its back in camel-like fashion and hissed. The Aborigine noticed that there was an unusually large number of flies about. A small boy came out of the door:—

"Hello, Yurgama," he greeted.

"Good day, Clarry. Where did all the flies come from?"

"Dad's got a heap of fowl manure for the garden. No doubt the flies have increased from that. We've managed to keep them out of the main part of the house. But they've managed to get into one room. Do you know, Yurgama, I've killed seven flies with the one swat."

"I don't believe you," said the Trooper.

"Come into the room and watch me."

In the room where there were many flies, young Clarry would wait till they settled on a wall, then strike. Before Yurgama's eyes, the boy killed not just seven, but eight flies with the one swat.

The Trooper went over the paddocks to see the lad's older brother Glen, and find out if everything was going well. He helped Glen all day and stayed for the evening meal.

Eventually, the Reid's cat was to find out that there was nothing to fear from Marakorpa. When the dingo squatted down majestically, the tabby walked over nervously and sniffed the bigger animal's nose. Seeing that Marakorpa was docile, the cat repeatedly walked under the dingo's neck and around his body.

After the late evening dinner, Glen asked his younger brother to get ready for bed.

"Not yet, Glen," complained Clarry, "I want Yurgama to talk to me for a while."

"Okay," relented the older boy.

The young lad was seated with the Trooper in armchairs in the Reid living room. The boy stared at the Aborigine till he became uncomfortable.

"Well what do you want to talk about, Clarry?" asked the lawman, wanting to break the silence.

"Yurgama, why is your skin black and ours is white?"

"People in different parts of the world have different coloured skins, Clarry. Why that came to be so, I don't know."

"Do any people or animals live on the stars?"

"I don't know, Clarry."

"What does God look like?"

"Oh, I couldn't tell you that."

"Were Adam and Eve really the first man and lady to live in the world?"

"I couldn't tell you that either."

Around nine o'clock that night, Yurgama overheard Clarry saying his prayers.

"God forgive me for being a bad boy. Please bless Mum and Dad, Glen and Yurgama. And God, let Yurgama know I don't mind him not knowing much."

Wiwirremalde

For many years, Bernie McDavitt operated a shoe repairing business in Tilabrook. When his son Lance grew up, Bernie took him into the business and taught him the trade. Then Bernie contracted a rare fatal disease. For much time, he was in considerable pain and bedridden. Doctor Eric Wudder declared to Lance that nothing could be done for his father. He could not be saved.

Lance became desperate. He was willing to gamble on attempting to attain help for his father from anything or anybody.

An acquaintance told him about a wandering Aboriginal mystic who taught himself to read and write and had the ability to correctly foretell future events. Among his prominent forecasts were the fact that he had predicted long before it happened, that the Burke and Wills party would not return from their journey through central Australia. Similarly, he had said the miners at Ballarat would rise at the Eureka Stockade. They would lose their battle with the Troopers, but win their rights. This forecast was made long before the event took place, too.

More importantly, where Lance was concerned, the acquaintance informed him that the mystic had cured many of the sick and ailing members of Aboriginal tribes by the laying on of his hands. In his wanderings, white settlers came to offer him lodging and food, because he cured members of their families and friends. The Aborigines called him Wiwirremalde.

Lance McDavitt had no hesitation in spending much of his life savings to pay to bring Wiwirremalde from north Queensland where he had been living at the time. It took an anguishing long time to first find out the mystic's whereabouts. He finally arrived in Tilabrook when Bernie McDavitt was near death's door.

The black man was dressed in a brown robe. He had long white hair, wore a long white beard and carried a staff. Lance anxiously took him to his father's bed.

Dramatically, Wiwirremalde concentrated for a long moment, closed his eyes in brief meditation and prayer, then laid his fingers on the head of Bernie McDavitt.

Within a week, Bernie made a gradual and astounding recovery to full health.

He and Lance insisted on the mystic being their guest for a few weeks. During this time, many people, like Eric Wudder, came to have discussions and listen to Wiwirremalde.

The part of the year was autumn. The weather was exceedingly pleasant. One day, the McDavitt father and son asked their Aboriginal guest if he would like to accompany them in their wagon for a picnic and hike in the bush.

The Flatterys lived next door to the McDavitts in Tilabrook and Bernie invited young Neville to come. To add to the party, Yurgama was invited to come too, and he brought Marakorpa along.

While the men enjoyed their food and beverage near a remote creek, Neville showed the adults his prowess with a well-made shanghai. He placed three small empty tobacco tins on a rock. And from a long distance, he knocked each of the tins down with three stones catapulted from his slingshot.

Once everyone's appetites were satisfied, the party took the hike along the creek. Neville walked ahead of the adults and Marakorpa took intermittent swims in the creek.

After walking for some time, most of the party sat down to take a rest. Neville was the only member still feeling energetic and desirous of staying on his feet.

In this period, Lance McDavitt drew everyone's attention to a handsome hawk in a tree. Then, while they admired the bird, Yurgama saw that Neville was standing below the tree preparing to take a shot at the hawk with his shanghai.

The black Trooper drew his arkana from his belt and threw it. Just before the boy catapulted a stone from the slingshot, the boomerang cut the rubber and returned to the Aborigine.

"Yurgama, you've busted the shanghai," said Neville, disappointedly looking at his sling shot.

"Sorry about that, mate," apologised the Trooper.

"I could have brought that hawk down," continued the boy.

Wiwirremalde helped Yurgama to persuade Neville not to want to kill birds with his shanghai.

Some discussion was held to find out if anyone wanted to conclude the hike. But everyone desired to continue for a while.

They walked another mile, when Marakorpa, in one of his swims in the creek, confronted a platypus.

The dingo growled aggressively at the duckbill.

Yurgama tossed his arkana across the creek.

Like a flat stone, the implement bounced over the water between Marakorpa and the platypus before it bounced back to the Trooper.

But it failed to divide the animals as Yurgama intended.

Marakorpa attempted to attack and the duckbill struck out defensively with its claw. The poison from the animal's claw went into the dingo's bloodstream causing him to yelp.

Yurgama dived into the water with his clothes on and brought his pained pet back to land as quickly as he could.

Bernie and Lance McDavitt looked inquiringly at Wiwirremalde. Though they did not say it, the mystic understood that they were wondering if he could heal Marakorpa.

He declared that he had never attempted to cure an animal, but he would try now.

On the suffering dingo, he carried out the same dignified ritual he had performed on Bernie McDavitt.

Marakorpa had to be carried back to the wagon, but like Bernie, he incredibly recovered to good health.

Wiwirremalde commented that the dingo was highly intelligent and could have sensed, the same way as people, that it was his intention to try and heal him.

"Wiwirremalde, have you ever failed to cure people?" asked Lance.

"Yes, some people have failed to respond," answered the Aborigine.

On the outskirts of the western part of Tilabrook, there lived a retired squatter and his wife. The squatter requested Wiwirremalde to come and stay at his home and try to cure his wife. She had taken a stroke and had become paralysed in the right arm as a result.

When the black mystic left the McDavitts to go to this couple's home, Bernie, Lance and Yurgama farewelled him.

Bernie asked, "What is the future of life, Wiwirremalde? Are we doomed to be born, to struggle, suffer and die?"

"Never despair, Bernie," answered the Aborigine. The day will come when the universe will become a place of eternal peace, safety, freedom, harmony, goodness and happiness for all life that has ever lived."

A shocked Bernie McDavitt turned to Yurgama after Wiwirremalde smiled and left them.

"Is he right?" asked the older McDavitt.

"I hope so," replied the Trooper as they watched the mystic walk away into the sunset.

Son of Convicts

One of the chestnut's shoes had become loose. Yurgama used a rock as an improvised hammer to nail the shoe back onto the horse's hoof. He was in ironbark bushland ten miles out of Tilabrook on a cool spring day.

The Trooper was distracted from the task, when he noticed a rider reining in his bay gelding not far off.

An annoyed magpie was making noise in the vicinity. It must have had a nest. Unexpectedly, the bird swooped down on the rider.

Yurgama whipped his arkana from his belt and threw it. Before returning to him, the implement struck and killed the magpie when the bird was only inches above the top of the rider's head.

The surprised man asked the Aborigine the reason for his action, to which Yurgama answered that he averted the probability of him getting a nasty wound to the head.

"I've just been pondering on the thought to make a fire here and boil a billy for some tea. What about joining me?" invited the man, dismounting.

"Yes, I will. Thanks a lot," accepted Yurgama. But when the Aborigine had his back turned for a minute to tighten his saddle girth, and was telling the man that the mate of the magpie he killed would look after their young, the fellow hit the Trooper in the back of the head with his rifle butt.

Yurgama came to consciousness an hour later, when his aggressor poured water over his face. The Aborigine felt a headache and found himself to be tied up to the bottom of a tree.

"While you were asleep, I went through your saddlebag, Trooper. I learnt you assisted in the escort of £2000 worth of gold from Heathcote to Tilabrook recently. And you're to see it safely escorted further to Melbourne from the Bank of NSW in Tilabrook," declared the man.

Yurgama said nothing.

"You're the same build as me," continued the fellow. "So your uniform should fit me perfectly. What I have in mind is to knock you out again and strip you. Then tomorrow morning, I'll go to the Tilabrook Bank and tell them I've been assigned to escort the gold to the city in your unexpected absence."

"Do you think they will believe you without official papers?" cautioned Yurgama.

"Yes. I'll tell them you've sent me. And if you think I'm really ruthless, I want you to know I intend telling them where you are, in case you have difficulties getting back to town and the care of a Doctor. Of course, I'll be far away with the gold by then.

"Sorry, but you will have to spend the night where you are. But it shouldn't be too cold. I'll be cooking some food soon. If I have much left, over, I'll give some to you and your dog. I think he's been puzzled by the situation," remarked the man, referring to Marakorpa.

"Why do you turn to crime to make a living?" asked Yurgama.

"You ask me that, Trooper," reacted the fellow. "Well, I'll

tell you a hard luck story. My parents were convicts under the Reverend Samuel Marsden in Sydney. Marsden had my father hung and my mother flogged. He slave worked my mother. And on occasions, she did not receive adequate pay or the bare necessities of life. Consequently, I sometimes went days without food, because she had nothing to give me. I don't intend to ever starve again, if I can help it."

When night fell, there was a bright half moon in the sky. Hence, it was easy to see in the dark. Through discomfort and stiffness, Yurgama was unable to get any sleep. Marakorpa was wandering around and the man's fire had gone out. He had bedded down for the night and had slumbered into a deep sleep. The Aborigine noticed that the resting fellow had left the arkana with his gear.

"Korp! Come here!" called the Trooper softly to his dingo.

Marakorpa came up with his tongue out and tail wagging.

"Fetch the arkana, Boy!" instructed the Aborigine.

At first, the dingo stood where he was, unsure, till the instruction was repeated.

He at last went quietly over and picked up the steel-rimmed boomerang in his mouth. He brought it back and put it down on the ground near his Master.

After much effort, Yurgama managed to manoeuvre the implement into a position where he could rub the rope against the steel.

With perseverance and time, the Aborigine cut the rope through. But when the task was nearly completed, the man stirred in his sleep, awoke and saw his victim getting free. He ran straight to his tethered gelding to get his rifle.

Perspiration was trickling down Yurgama's face as he made an all out effort to quickly cut the last strands of rope.

Just as the man was about to reach for his rifle, the Aborigine, now free, despairingly grabbed his arkana and tossed it. The implement slashed the fellow's hand. His instant thought was immediate escape and he mounted his horse without giving attention to his bleeding hand.

But before the fellow could escape into the night, Yurgama threw his returned arkana hard. The implement cut the horse's reins after the man had dug his boots into its belly. The gelding reacted obediently and tore off. But with the reins broken, the fellow had no control over his hack. He fell from it and was killed instantly—his neck getting broken in the fall.